The Challenge

The steady rumble of fists hitting the speedbags inside the Brooklyn Athletic Club followed Diana as she made her way to the office of Hector, the trainer.

As she neared the door she saw Hector playing dominoes with two men. He looked up and smiled. "You here to beat me up?"

"No . . . I'm here cuz—"

"See her the other day?" Hector asked the other men, chuckling. "Bare-knuckled! You should've seen Ray's face."

"I wanna train with you," Diana said slowly to Hector. "I wanna be a boxer."

Hector started to shuffle the dominoes. "I'm not interested in training girls. Besides, there's plenty of things you can do better with your life than box."

"Yeah?" Diana said quietly. "Prove it."

MEDIA TIE-INS

girlfight

A Novelization by Frank Lauria
Based on the Motion Picture Written and Directed
by Karyn Kusama

POCKET BOOKS
New York London Toronto Sydney Singapore

This book is a work of fiction. Names, characters, places and incidents are products of the author's imagination or are used fictitiously. Any resemblance to actual events or locales or persons, living or dead, is entirely coincidental.

An *Original* Publication of POCKET BOOKS

POCKET BOOKS, a division of Simon & Schuster, Inc.
1230 Avenue of the Americas, New York, NY 10020

ISBN: 0-7434-1905-7

First Pocket Books printing October 2000

10 9 8 7 6 5 4 3 2 1

POCKET and colophon are registered trademarks of Simon & Schuster, Inc.

Printed in the U.S.A.

girlfight

Chapter 1

Brooklyn is another country.

It has its own slang, its own style of rap, its own street code. But some things are the same everywhere.

Between classes at Eleanor Roosevelt Public High School, the girls' rest room was a beehive of frantic activity. Teenaged girls stood two-deep at the mirrors. They fixed their hair, refreshed their makeup, and talked about boys.

Their noisy chatter bounced off the cracked tile walls as Diana Guzman stepped inside. She peered across the jammed, smoke-hazed room looking for her best friend, Marisol.

As Diana shouldered her way through the crowd

she caught her reflection in the spotted mirror. Her hair was braided close to her head in tight corn-rows that framed her striking features. She was taller than most of the students crowding around her. But it was the intense, slightly threatening, glint in her eyes that parted the girls in her path.

She moved to the far wall and hoisted herself onto the windowsill with catlike ease. "Marisol!" Diana called out, raising her voice above the din.

"I'm here!" Marisol called back.

At the moment Marisol was in one of the stalls, engaged in an argument with Veronica, who was standing in front of the mirrors. It was no contest. Veronica was beautiful, and sharp as a cobra's fangs. Marisol wore braces and still carried some baby fat.

"It's a free country, Marisol," Veronica purred, her attention fixed on her own reflection. "Just cuz you have a crush on him doesn't mean you *own* him."

Veronica's ever-present girlfriends snickered.

Marisol ignored them as she exited the stall. "You didn't even notice him till you found out I liked him," she said lamely, wishing she hadn't.

Veronica rolled her eyes. "Please—get *over* your-self." Then she glimpsed Diana glaring at her and stiffened. Everybody knew Diana was trouble.

The boy in question was Terrance Hernandez. He was tall, dark, gawky, and shy. Marisol had found out that Terrance wanted to be a songwriter, a dream she shared. The two of them would meet in the auditorium after school to try to pick out tunes on the tinny piano. One day Terrance stopped coming. A week later Marisol found out why. He was too busy panting after Veronica like a hound at a hot-dog stand.

"It's true," Marisol whined. "You can have any guy you want and you choose him."

Veronica paused, savoring her victory. She glanced at her admirers, then heaved a long sigh. "Nothing happened," she assured Marisol, dabbing her own lips with a tissue. "Can we be friends now?"

Veronica's girlfriends smiled knowingly. Marisol stared at Veronica, wanting desperately to believe her. She opened her mouth to speak.

Diana hopped off the windowsill. "You fucked him."

"I did not!" Veronica snapped. But she became nervous when she saw Diana advancing toward her.

Every girl in the rest room turned to watch.

"You're lying," Diana accused coldly, eyes fixed on Veronica.

Veronica met her stare. "I am not," she insisted. But her words didn't ring true. A second later she glanced away. And everybody knew.

Marisol felt as if she'd been shot. "You had sex with him?"

Veronica angrily jabbed her finger at Diana. "Guzman, you suck! It didn't mean anything—as if it's your business."

"That's really bitchy . . ." Marisol croaked, trying to recover her poise.

Veronica spun around. "*Hey*—you can't talk that shit to me." She gave Marisol a nasty smile. "So Terrance prefers me over you, is that my problem? Maybe it's time you looked in the mirror, Marisol. Time for a make-over, know what I'm saying?"

Marisol shrank back, mortified by the other girls' mocking laughter.

Diana's anger flared at the sight of her friend being taunted. She thrust herself in front of Marisol and got in Veronica's face. "Tell her you're sorry."

"Excuse *me?*" Veronica asked in disbelief. She tried to appear cool, but the fury in Diana's eyes unnerved her.

"You heard me," Diana repeated. "Apologize to her."

"Yeah, right . . ." Veronica said, trying to save face. She turned and walked to the door, her friends trailing behind.

Still seething, Veronica marched out to the busy hallway and joined the students hurrying to their next class. She didn't look back or she would have seen Diana stalking her like a hungry lioness.

"I'm telling you. She's *psy-cho,*" Veronica announced to her girlfriends.

Diana didn't really hear the remark. Her skull was howling with rage as she drew closer and suddenly pounced, tackling Veronica to the floor.

Scratching and kicking furiously, both girls rolled on the ground. Instantly, a crowd of students circled the writhing pair. "Kill her, mommy, kill her!" someone yelled.

A passing girl student gave the scene a bored glance. "Jesus. American Gladiators."

Diana's younger brother, Tiny, tried to push through the rowdy spectators. He knew his sister's temper could explode like dynamite, but he didn't want Diana to get expelled. Then the crowd parted, and he saw Diana scrambling on top of Veronica.

With a triumphant snarl Diana grabbed a fistful

of Veronica's hair and prepared to smack her head against the floor.

Mr. Price stopped her just in time. The lanky teacher pulled Diana off, and Veronica scrambled to her feet, hair disheveled and makeup smeared. Still holding Diana at bay, Mr. Price turned to the onlookers. "Show's over. You kids are late to class."

No one moved. The teacher's expression hardened. "I said hustle!" Mr. Price barked. "Or *all* of you end up in detention."

Silently, the crowd melted away, but Tiny and Marisol lingered for a moment. "See ya . . ." Tiny whispered. Diana glanced at him as if surprised. Marisol caught Diana's eye and dramatically mouthed the words "call me." Then Tiny and Marisol retreated down the hall, leaving Mr. Price with his delinquent females.

Breath heaving, Veronica glared at Diana. "You are fucking *crazy!*" she ranted hysterically.

"You started it," Diana taunted her.

Veronica's jaw dropped in disbelief. "Mr. Price, she is *lying*—I did not do *anything.*"

"You know what you did—" Diana struggled to get loose, but the teacher tightened his grip.

"Enough!" Mr. Price warned. "You're in detention for the next two weeks. Both of you."

"But, Mr. Price, I didn't do nothing!" Veronica wailed.

Diana made a face. " 'Cept be your skanky, stinky self."

"Quiet!" Mr. Price ordered. "Until I get the facts you are both at fault. Don't report after school today—and you're suspended." He glared at them to make sure they understood. Then he released his hold on Diana. "Now get to class."

Veronica shot a last, venomous glance at Diana, then turned and moved stiffly down the hall.

Mr. Price grabbed Diana's arm before she could follow. "You." The teacher sighed wearily. "You're another story."

The principal's outer office had nothing but a hard wooden bench to sit on. Mr. Price and Diana waited uncomfortably while the principal finished a drawn-out phone conversation. Slightly depressed after the adrenaline rush of combat, Diana was resigned to her fate. She usually tried to control her temper, but the rage came over her like a tidal wave, sweeping her up with it. Diana didn't know where the boiling anger came from, but it was starting to worry her. And she sure didn't need to get expelled from school so near graduation.

"Ms. Martinez will see you now," the secretary announced.

Diana got up and walked into the office. Right behind her, Mr. Price rolled his eyes at the secretary, as if to say "See what I have to contend with around here." The secretary gave him a long-suffering smile. As he passed her desk he whispered, "Animals."

The principal's desk was stacked with papers. When they were seated, Ms. Martinez ran her finger down the student roster. "Guzman, Ernesto," she murmured, using Tiny's given name. Then she paused and looked up. "Guzman . . . Diana."

Diana slouched in her chair. She knew what was coming.

"It's your fourth fight this semester. You simply can't continue to behave like this," Ms. Martinez intoned sternly.

Diana stared at the carpet, scuffing at it with her tennis shoe.

Ms. Martinez glanced over Diana's academic record: above average grades, every semester. She could actually qualify for college. But the principal

8

knew that even graduation from high school was a rare achievement in Red Hook, Brooklyn.

"You're bright," Ms. Martinez said, softening her tone. "You get decent grades despite your attitude. But this discipline problem is completely out of control."

"It was her fault," Diana mumbled.

"Have you considered how much more effective it would be to talk about your disagreement?" the principal suggested.

Marisol tried that and see where it got her, Diana thought. She looked at Ms. Martinez and shrugged. "Talk? With Veronica? You've gotta be kidding."

"Fighting with her isn't the answer," Ms. Martinez snapped. "You have a serious problem. In school or out, your life is only going to get harder because of it. You might want to find someone who can help you deal with this."

"I don't need any help," Diana said defensively. She didn't need some weirdo shrink. Ms. Martinez didn't know what happened to people in her hood who backed down.

Ms. Martinez looked at Diana for a moment, then checked her watch. She had done what she could. She was an administrator, not a psychiatrist.

"Fine. It's up to you. I'm out of options," she told Diana flatly. "One more fight and you're expelled."

"Who cares if I'm expelled?" Diana blurted.

"Diana—ask *yourself* that question."

Diana looked away. She already had.

Diana lived in a tall, concrete box that looked exactly the same as the other six boxes that made up the housing project. The buildings were clustered around two concrete parks with a few trees thrown in for effect.

It was nearly dark when Diana got home. It was a toss-up which was worse, the dark, dangerous stairs or the rickety elevator. Luckily the elevator was waiting for her. Diana got off on the eleventh floor and walked down the graffiti-scrawled hallway to her apartment.

She could hear music and loud laughter inside. Her father was gambling with his pals, as usual. Diana turned the key in the lock and tried to open the door. Chained from the inside. Diana smacked the door hard with her palm. A child began to cry somewhere down the hall. She banged the door again.

"Who is it?"

She recognized the voice of her father's friend Edward. "Diana—open up."

She heard the chain rattle, and Edward opened the door. He nodded at her. "Hey there. It's Diana!" he announced cheerfully.

Diana heard her father's voice behind him. "She's late."

Edward gave her a weary smile and stepped back. Diana followed him to the living room, where three men were playing cards on a fold-out table. The room smelled of beer, sweat, and tobacco. Flashlights and construction equipment lay in a heap on the floor. *Probably just came from a sewer,* Diana thought. She wished they'd all go away.

Sandro, Diana's father, glanced up at her. "The gym's probably closed by now."

Diana wasn't sure what he was talking about. And she didn't care.

"Got held up at school," she muttered.

Sandro lifted his eyes. "You in trouble?"

"No," Diana said automatically.

Sandro handed her some folded bills. "Tell Hector I'll have the rest next week."

"Not after this game," Edward warned.

Diana leaned over to see her father's cards. Sandro covered them up. He didn't like his daughter hanging around the card table.

"Where am I going?" Diana asked, grateful for any excuse to be out of there.

"The gym. Take the Sixty-one to York. It's near the water."

Edward seemed shocked. "Why you send your girl down there?"

"She's paying Hector. My good man from Panama is training Tiny."

"These kids on the street now . . ." Edward muttered, examining his cards.

"*Hijo,* I know it," Sandro said, tossing a bill on the table. "I'm investing in my son's future."

Sure won't catch him investing in his daughter's future, Diana thought. As she turned to go, Edward smiled up at her.

"You are the living likeness of your mother, may she rest in peace . . ."

"Hey, hey—" Sandro said sharply.

"What?" Edward said indignantly. "I was just sayin'—"

Sandro gave Edward a hard glare, and he stopped talking.

Her father rarely mentioned her mother since

her death, and Diana knew why. She felt the anger
build up inside as she headed for the door.

"Later," Diana said over her shoulder. Her father
didn't respond. She could hear the card game resume behind her. It was like she had never been
there.

"Be careful," Edward called.

"Don't worry about me," Diana said sarcastically.
But nobody heard.

Chapter 2

The slate gray warehouses along the waterfront loomed like tombstones in a deserted graveyard as Diana walked slowly toward the fluorescent lights at the end of the long, dark street.

As she neared the club, she could hear the constant drumming of many fists pounding speedbags. Like an army marching. Louis, the doorman at the Brooklyn Athletic Club, saw her coming through half-closed lids. It was his job to screen entrants to the large warehouse that served as a boxing gym. He didn't like girls coming to the gym. Girls were always trouble. He'd tell her no women allowed. Louis closed his eyes and waited for her to come closer. . . .

The old man sitting at the door seemed to be asleep. But as Diana approached, he lifted his eyes.

"I'm looking for Hector," Diana said.

Louis shrugged as if disappointed. He jerked his thumb at the stairway and closed his eyes again. Diana went inside and climbed to the second floor.

The boxing gym was a noisy, run-down place. There was a raised boxing ring in the back, six heavy bags in the center, and four speedbags aligned against the water-stained walls. The heavy odor of sweat, blood, and industrial detergent hung in the damp air. The pay phone in the corner kept ringing until somebody nearby answered. A few seconds after he hung up it started ringing again. A constant series of mechanized bells went off every sixty seconds.

Trying not to seem flustered, Diana searched the crowded gym for her brother, Tiny. Boxers of all sizes and shapes were at work: pounding the bags, skipping rope, shadowboxing, sparring, under the watchful eyes of trainers. Diana was slightly jealous. She never got lessons in anything from her father. It wasn't really Tiny's fault. Her father believed females were born to be housewives.

A good-looking young man shadowboxing near the wall caught Diana's attention. He was a year or so older than Diana, and slim, with long muscles that moved fluidly under his glistening skin. His trainer sat against the wall, making comments.

Diana watched for a few moments. The young boxer circled like a dancer. Then he threw a flurry of punches, and she saw his speed and power.

"Good, very good," the trainer called.

The final bell sounded and the young boxer paused. He lifted his head and saw Diana staring. For an instant their eyes met. Diana quickly turned away and began moving toward the back of the gym.

Diana approached a teenaged boxer who was awkwardly jumping rope. His trainer stood nearby, leaning on a cane. The trainer wore a yellow bowling shirt with the name *Don* embroidered on the front. A brimmed straw hat seemed permanently planted on his head. Without warning Don lifted his cane and swung it hard at the boxer's legs.

The boxer leaped high, narrowly avoiding a bruised shin.

"You need some *variety,* and I give it to you," Don said, cackling. Then he saw Diana and paused, looking her over. "Yeah?"

"I got something for Hector."

Don nodded. "The ring in the back." He returned his attention to his boxer.

As Diana neared the raised boxing ring, she saw a crowd of men and boys gathered to watch two young fighters sparring. One of the fighters was Tiny. Tiny was smaller and seemed younger than his opponent, a stocky brawler with a nasty face. Diana's brother, on the other hand, had the innocent features of a choirboy, and his thin, agile body was more suited to dancing than fighting. Tiny's quickness kept frustrating his heavier, slower opponent.

A man who looked much older than her father leaned on the ropes, shouting instructions at Tiny. Diana assumed the man was Hector. He peered over his reading glasses at the fighters with an intent, almost puzzled expression, as if he was trying to solve some tricky problem.

Diana moved through the crowd and stood beside him. Hector kept watching the pair in the ring. "Remember your combinations, Tiny," he shouted.

It didn't matter. Tiny needed a gun in there. He was hopelessly mismatched. His opponent kept throwing punches while Tiny ducked and bobbed, never punching back. The warning bell rang—sixty seconds left.

"Last round," Hector called out.

The stocky fighter drove Tiny back with a rapid combination. "You said we'd go for three," he protested.

"He's not ready," Hector declared.

Tiny kept ducking and weaving, aware the ordeal was almost over.

The bell sounded and Tiny dropped his hands. But the stocky fighter kept swinging. As Tiny started to remove his headgear the other fighter popped him in the face. Hector threw his hands up in disgust.

"Where the hell is Don?" Hector shouted.

Still wobbly on his feet, Tiny climbed out of the ring. Diana saw the trainer with the cane approaching. Hector glared at Don and jabbed a finger at the stocky fighter still inside the ring. "If this bozo's your guy, you should keep an eye on him."

"Ray?" the trainer protested. "Ray don't listen to a word I say."

Hector leaned closer. "*Make* him listen."

Meanwhile, Ray was pumping his fists in the air in a lame show of victory. Then he removed his headgear and climbed out of the ring. As he moved past Diana, she touched his arm. When he turned, Diana swung wildly. Her fist swatted his jaw, and he stepped back, stunned.

Ray blinked at Diana. "What the fuck—"

"That's my *brother*, you little shit!"

Ray lunged at her, but Don grabbed him from behind. "Ray! Easy!" The trainer took Ray's arm and pulled him back toward the locker room.

"I gotta put you in a cage from now on?" Don growled.

Ray glared back at Diana. "The ho' hit me first!"

"I'm talking about that cheap crap in the ring. When you gonna learn some decency?"

Diana saw Hector watching her. A few others had stopped to see the action. One of them was the good-looking young boxer Diana had noticed earlier. Their eyes met and he turned away. The other onlookers returned to their training.

Diana turned and saw her brother with Hector. The trainer held Tiny's face by the chin, while he examined the boy's nose. When Tiny saw Diana approaching he squirmed free. Normally her brother had a sweet nature, but at the moment he was outraged.

"Girl! You are so *embarrassing*," Tiny declared.

"Twice in a day makes me look like a pussy."

"Watch your mouth," Hector warned.

But Tiny wasn't finished with Diana. "Why'd you mess with Ray like that?"

"He's a punk, Tiny."

"We were sparring!"

"Didn't look that way to me," Diana said, but she knew what Tiny meant. She turned to Hector and handed him the money. "This is from my dad."

The trainer seemed surprised. "You're Sandro's kid? How come I never heard of you?"

"I don't know—I'm his pride and joy," Diana said evenly.

Hector didn't get the joke. There was an awkward pause. "Nice meeting you," Diana said finally.

Hector shrugged. "Yeah."

Diana found a bench and waited while Tiny showered and changed into his street clothes. Her anger receded as she watched the fighters training. She felt strangely at home in the spartan surroundings.

The good-looking young boxer Diana had seen earlier came out of the locker.

"Yo, Adrian, see you tomorrow," someone called. The young boxer waved and kept going.

Adrian—so that's his name, Diana thought, watching him leave.

Adrian felt tired and hungry. He paused on the stairwell and took a lollipop from his pocket. He wasn't supposed to eat candy, but he had worked out hard tonight. He deserved a treat.

Then he saw Ray sitting on the stairs and decided to play him a little. "You've been humiliated, *hijo*," Adrian said with mock sadness. "You fight dirty with a li'l kid and then get slapped by a *girl?* That's weak."

"That bitch is lucky I didn't kill her," Ray muttered.

Adrian nodded solemnly. "You spared her some mighty force, huh?"

Ray laughed. "That's right."

They fell silent when they saw who was coming upstairs—Karina, a young woman of about twenty, very attractive, with a body that was straight out of *Vogue.* She had long straight hair and exotic almond-shaped eyes. Her long nails, tight dress, and high heels were perfect and in sharp contrast to her present surroundings. She gave Adrian a smile as she passed. Adrian smiled back.

As he watched Karina go inside the gym, Adrian

saw the girl who'd punched Ray coming out. The girl wasn't as stylish as Karina, far from it. But she carried herself with a kind of proud grace. Even without makeup or fancy clothes there was something really deep and beautiful about her, especially her eyes.

Adrian recognized the young guy with her. Tiny was one of Hector's boys.

"Who's the dish?" Adrian asked casually, hoping Ray would be cool. Of course he wasn't.

"Should have me a taste and find out," Ray said, loud enough for the girl to hear.

Adrian swatted at him, slightly embarrassed.

As Tiny and the girl came near, Ray called out, "Hey, little man—you know I'm just playing."

Tiny shrugged as if it didn't matter. "I know."

"Can we shake?"

Slowly Tiny extended his hand. As Ray moved to take it, Tiny snatched his hand back and ran it through his hair. "Thought you had a friend."

Adrian smiled. The kid was cool.

Ray gave Tiny a semifriendly shove and they shook hands for real. Then Ray turned to Diana. "Hey, killer, I forgive you, too."

Diana wasn't amused. "Oh, yeah?" she challenged him.

Ray lifted his hands in mock surrender. "Guess you never learned how to be a lady."

Diana snorted in disgust, but Ray had stung her.

"You shouldn't hit people like that," Adrian put in.

Diana turned and saw Adrian smiling at her. She glanced at Ray. "I couldn't resist," she said, suddenly anxious to leave. "Tiny! Let's go."

Later Diana wondered why she had been in such a hurry to go home.

As usual the dinner table was a war zone. Tiny and Diana sat across from each other, eating their dinner. Sandro sat dourly at the head of the table, drinking a beer.

Tiny broke the silence. "Got that scholarship application I told you about," he announced proudly.

Diana perked up at the news. "For the art school?"

"Yeah—it's cool. You gotta learn all kinds of stuff before you even do the work you want, to get a foundation."

"You *would* think that's cool." As soon as Diana said it she wished she hadn't. She knew how much his artwork meant to Tiny—and how hard their father made it for Tiny to keep his dream alive.

"Sounds like a waste of time to me," Sandro said.

"Learn how to draw, what's that get you? A job painting somebody's big house on Long Island!"

Tiny's enthusiasm vanished. "Maybe."

Diana glanced at her father. "Edward clean you out like he said?"

"He screws himself when he talks like that."

Her father's scowl told Diana he had lost. They sat in silence for long minutes. Finally Diana got up and started to take her plate to the sink.

Sandro glared at her. "I'm not finished."

"I know," Diana said half-defiantly. She moved into the kitchen.

Sandro turned to his son and smiled. "How was school today, champ?"

Never talks to me that way, Diana brooded, putting her plate in the sink.

"School was okay," Tiny said casually. "Lots of excitement."

Diana shot her brother a warning glance. She needn't have worried; her father didn't get Tiny's meaning. He was on one of his trips down memory lane.

"Lucky you," Sandro droned. "When I was a kid, school was so boring I thought I'd piss in my pants, waiting to get out in the world."

"Did it happen?" Diana's question was barbed with contempt.

"What?"

"Did you get 'out in the world'?"

Sandro's eyes narrowed. "I met your mother, we had you two," he said, as if that explained everything. But Diana knew she'd hit a nerve. She also knew that any second he might lash out in rage. The way he used to with her mother.

The phone's ringing broke the tension. Tiny jumped up to answer it. Sandro continued staring at his daughter as if she were a stranger.

"What kind of question is that?"

"Dad!" Tiny called from the other room.

Sandro left the table and went to answer the phone. Diana could hear the low, angry rumble of his voice in the next room. Tiny hurried back into the kitchen.

"It's Ms. Martinez," he whispered. Then he headed for his room and closed the door behind him. Even without seeing him, Diana was sure he had picked up his sketchbook, knowing he could shut out the world with his pen.

Diana stood tense, ready to defend herself physically. But when her father came back he just stood there, glowering like a confused bull.

"That was a lady from the school. She says you attacked a student. Gave some rap about family therapy," Sandro added with disgust, as if she had suggested eating rats. He shook his head wearily. "Why you always got to fuck up like this?"

"Veronica asked for it!"

Sandro walked out of the kitchen, shaking his head. "You embarrass me," he said over his shoulder. "I don't even think you're *mine* sometimes."

"Maybe I'm not!" Diana snapped, but he pretended not to hear. Her father's icy indifference hurt worse than his fists ever could. Diana stood alone in the kitchen, wet plate clutched against her chest like a shield.

Then the fury burst through. Without warning Diana lifted the plate and shattered it against the floor. Seconds later her father appeared in the doorway.

He stared at her as if she were a rare animal in a zoo. No anger, no compassion, just cold curiosity. Sandro shrugged and pointed to the floor.

"Now you have to clean it up."

He turned and went into the other room. Diana smacked her fist on the counter, but he didn't respond. Jaw clenched, she went to the closet and got the broom and dustpan. She heard the front door to the apartment open and close. Her father had gone out.

"Fuck you . . ." she whispered in the empty kitchen.

Detention was a total drag.

Diana sat on one side of the room, Veronica on another, with a few other detainees in between. A teacher sat at the front desk, grading papers.

Diana tried to study, but it was no use. Like everybody else she kept watching the clock. She glanced over at her enemy. Veronica was flipping through a fashion magazine she'd been smart enough to bring. Every three seconds she would examine her long, purple fingernails.

Diana got a sinking feeling when she saw Mr. Price peer in through the door's window. He came inside, whispered something to the teacher, then motioned to Veronica. "Bring your stuff," he told her.

Veronica flashed a triumphant smile as she hustled past Diana's desk. They both knew why Mr. Price was there. Witnesses had told the teacher what had happened. Now Diana had to serve her detention alone. Diana groaned softly and stared at the clock.

Finally the bell set her free.

Diana hurried down the hall to the girls' lockers, where Marisol was waiting. The two girls left the school grounds and walked over to the Fulton Mall, their usual shopping hangout.

The Fulton Mall wasn't really a mall. It was a few city blocks blocked off to traffic, allowing pedestrians to shop freely at the chain of discount stores that lined both sides of the street. Most stores featured cut-rate clothing or cheap audio equipment. Blaring music from the electronics stores followed Diana and Marisol as they strolled the crowded street.

A shapely young woman wearing a nearly transparent dress sauntered past them. Marisol turned to stare.

"If I was enough of a skeez I could pull that off," Marisol said.

Diana kept walking. "Why would you want to?"

Easy for you to say, Marisol observed, hurrying to catch up. Diana had a great body under her sweatshirts and loose jeans. She just didn't care about that stuff. Not like Veronica and her girls.

"Veronica say anything to you?" Marisol asked casually.

"Huh, yeah, sure," Diana snorted. "If she wants to choke on her teeth. That girl's too busy talking with her mirror." She held out her palm and fluttered her eyelashes. "Ooooh, jus' a second, baby. Let me get made up just perfect so I can suck your dick—which is all I'm good for anyway."

Marisol giggled at Diana's dead-on impersonation. "C'mon, let it rest with her."

Diana heard something she didn't like. "How come?" she snapped.

"Cuz . . ." Marisol said carefully. "She can be bitchy—but that's not all she's about, you know?"

Diana gave her a disgusted look. "Some fucking loyalty."

"Don't be like that," Marisol pleaded.

Diana walked away. "She treats you like shit. Why would you want to take her side?"

"Diana, I don't take sides. Veronica don't even mean half the shit she says!" Marisol stopped short when she saw Diana's stony expression. "Look, I just want to be friends with everyone—that's the way I am."

Diana stood in the street and watched an ice

cream truck jingling closer. *Friends with every-one—good luck*, she thought.

"Well, I hate her," she said aloud. "That's the way I am."

Marisol reached out and gave Diana's hair an affectionate yank. "Fool."

Later, back in her empty apartment, Diana was still brooding about Marisol's attitude. *Girlfriend's self-esteem needs rehab*, she decided.

I'm not so smart, either, Diana observed, opening the refrigerator door. *I'm the one who got in trouble trying to defend Marisol.*

She made herself a sandwich, then picked up a textbook and went into the living room. She sprawled on the couch, flicked on the TV, and started to study for her history test.

As she read she could hear snatches of a newscast. ". . . set his estranged wife on fire, then fatally shot himself. Neighbors of the slain woman expressed shock and sorrow . . ."

Without looking at the screen, Diana hit the remote. ". . . but, Scottie, after what we've been through together, I'd do anything for you. Don't you know that by now?"

Diana hit the remote again. "Active families can really make a mess. So when I need to get to the tough dirt I use . . ."

Diana switched off the TV and tried to study in silence. She managed to get through a half-hour before tossing the textbook aside. She felt strangely nervous, as if something was building inside of her. She prowled around the empty apartment for a while. Then, abruptly, she realized exactly what she wanted to do. And where she wanted to be.

She couldn't depend on anybody in this world. What she needed to do was learn how to depend on herself.

Diana bolted out the door and ran outside, where she caught the number 61 bus to the waterfront.

Chapter 3

The steady rumble of fists hitting the speed-bags inside the Brooklyn Athletic Club followed Diana as she made her way to Hector's office. As she neared the door she heard loud voices. Then someone shouted. She stopped and saw Hector seated at a table with two men, playing dominoes.

"Knock, knock . . ." Hector said, intent on the game.

Diana shrugged. "It was open."

Hector looked up and smiled. "You here to beat me up?"

"No . . . I'm here cuz—"

"See her the other day?" Hector asked the other

men, chuckling. "Bare-knuckled! You should've seen Ray's face."

Hector reenacted the scene in Spanish, making funny sound effects to accompany his mock punches. His pals laughed at his description of Ray trying to play tough guy.

"Hey!" Diana snapped. "I'm trying to say something."

All three men meekly put their hands over their mouths.

"I wanna train with you," Diana said slowly to Hector.

No one spoke. "I wanna be a boxer," she added.

"Sure," Hector murmured. "It's a great workout."

"No. For real. I wanna fight."

Hector glanced at his two friends. The fat one smiled uncomfortably. Hector shook his head. "I'll let you train, but you can't fight."

"Why not?" Diana demanded, struggling to keep her temper. It was always the same reason, but she wanted to hear him say it.

"You just *can't.* Girls don't have the power that boys do. It's just a fact."

"What about aerobics?" the fat man suggested.

Diana gave him a hard stare. "Am I talking to you?"

33

"Nice," the fat man muttered.

Diana turned back to Hector. "Look, I've been in fights all my life, and I think I've got some power."

Hector snorted. "You swiped Ray awful fast, and he deserved it. But this ain't no street brawl. There's *rules* to all this."

"Why do you think I'm here?" Diana pleaded. "I wanna learn from you."

"You box and you'll ruin your pretty face," the fat man warned.

Diana threw up her hands. "Aw, c'mon . . ."

The three men fell silent. Hector started to shuffle the dominoes. "Hey, I got enough kids on my plate. I'm just not interested in training girls. Besides, there's plenty of things you can do better with your life than box."

"Yeah?" Diana said quietly. "Prove it."

They all knew what she meant. There were very few life options in Red Hook, and most of them weren't very pretty. Boxing seemed almost respectable by comparison. It was even an Olympic sport—for boys.

Hector's friends watched expectantly as he shuffled the dominoes. Diana's plea had won them over,

34

but Hector still wasn't convinced. He saw them staring and heaved a weary sigh.

"You got money? Cuz I don't work for free."

"A little."

"I charge ten bucks a session. And that's cut-rate."

Diana's heart sank. This wasn't going to be easy. "I don't have that kind of cash," she told Hector.

Hector regarded her impassively. "So there you go."

Diana couldn't argue. They stared at each other for a moment. Then slowly Diana turned and walked out of the office.

Diana thought about what Hector had said all the way home.

That night during dinner, she brought it up to her father. "Dad? You know how you pay for Tiny to train with Hector?" she said carefully. "I was thinking how that's like an allowance, and, you know, that I should get an allowance, too."

"First off, it's not an allowance," her father corrected her.

Diana folded her arms. "Then what is it?"

"I'm preparing him. For the world out there."

I live in the world, too, Diana wanted to say, but

her father wasn't listening. As usual, he was making a sermon.

"It's insurance," Sandro explained, as if his reason was obvious. "You see how these boys are now—they want to eat him alive."

"That's not true—" Tiny blurted, slightly embarrassed. He could hold his own on the streets, despite his small size. But his father was always right.

"Tiny, it's *true*," Sandro said flatly.

"But what if he doesn't wanna box?" Diana suggested.

Tiny perked up, but his father scoffed at the idea. "Sure he wants to—what kid wouldn't?"

"He could go to college, Dad," Diana persisted. "He could do all sorts of stuff with himself."

Sensing he was losing ground, Sandro lashed out. "You think I don't know that? This isn't just spending money for your brother. He's not at A & S Plaza buying lipstick or whatever it is you girls do."

"Don't front like I'm some girly-girl when you know I'm not!" Diana shot back.

"Would it kill you to put on a skirt like everyone else?" Sandro said triumphantly.

No matter what I do—it's wrong, Diana thought. *What's the use of talking?*

"Your mother was a receptionist, and in a nice office, too," Sandro told her with a trace of pride. Then his voice hardened. "Get a job if you want extra money."

Diana shook her head slowly in disbelief.

Her father slapped the table. "I'm not giving you anything till you show me you deserve it."

"You don't give me anything, anyway," Diana said coldly. She stood up and went to her bedroom.

Diana didn't bother turning on the light. She stood in the darkness staring out the window. A girl her own age was walking across the courtyard below. Diana knew her by sight, but not by name. The girl was pushing a beat-up baby stroller. The toddler at her side was struggling to keep up the pace, but the girl didn't slow down.

Diana could see the girl was tired. When she spoke her voice sounded worn out and ragged. "Think I don't hear you crying?" she told the toddler. "I hear you all right."

Diana realized she had to fight for her dream, or she'd be swept under the rug like that girl, so early the next morning, while her father was taking a shower, Diana crept into his room. She opened his drawers, one by one, until she found a wool sock stuffed with an envelope. The envelope was filled with cash. Diana put three twenty-dollar bills into her pocket, then jammed the sock back into her father's drawer.

That afternoon detention went even more slowly than usual.

Diana drummed her fingers on the desk, watching the clock. The moment the bell rang she gathered her gear and ran out. She barely made the bus and settled gratefully into an empty window seat. Anticipation and nervousness churned through her thoughts. *I'm doing it, I'm really doing it,* she repeated, like a mantra.

As usual the old doorman at the Brooklyn Athletic Club seemed to be asleep, but when Diana came near he lifted his hand and waved her inside.

Maybe he's like a ninja doorman, Diana mused as she hurried upstairs. She slowed down when she reached the door. The gym seemed less crowded earlier in the day. Trying to control her eagerness, she walked calmly through the gym. She spotted Tiny working out with Hector at the rear of the gym.

Diana's heart skipped when she saw Adrian ahead. The young boxer was removing cloth wraps from his hands. He looked up and smiled.

"You again," he greeted her.

"Hi," Diana said casually as she passed. She liked his smile, but he made her nervous. She needed to focus on her mission.

Hector and Tiny paused, both gawking at her in surprise as she approached. "What are you doing here?" Tiny demanded.

Diana ignored him. "I got the money," she told Hector. She showed him the folded bills.

Hector looked away. "I didn't promise nothing."

A sudden flare of anger boiled through Diana's emotions. *Just like my father,* she raged inwardly. But she managed to keep her voice low and steady. "You said once I got the cash—"

Tiny gave her a warning stare. "Hey!"

"You seem like a nice kid," Hector said calmly.

"Diana!" Tiny persisted, wanting her to leave.

Hector paid no attention. "It's just not right," he told her, as if it were the eleventh commandment.

Frustration strained Diana's voice. "This is bullshit! You told me yes if I could pay. And now I can."

"You?" Tiny spun around in disbelief. "You're gonna train with Hector?"

"Yeah—I am," Diana said quietly.

"Why?" Tiny asked.

Diana shrugged. She had never really asked herself why. She just knew the first time she stepped inside the gym that she wanted to be a boxer. "Who's gonna protect me—you?" she said finally.

"What about Popi?"

Diana cocked her fists. "Tell Dad and I'll fucking kill you."

"Take it easy, okay?" Hector quickly stepped between them. "Christ . . ." He hesitated when he saw Diana's icy glare. *If somebody doesn't teach this kid right, she just might kill somebody,* he decided.

He gave Diana a weary smile. "I'll train you."

Diana's defensive scowl melted, and she looked like a kid at Christmas. "Yeah?"

Hector's expression turned deadly serious as he warned her, "If you don't sweat for me, you're outta my life. Got it?"

Diana relaxed. "I got it," she told Hector. "Thanks. Thank you."

"Aw, man . . ." Tiny lifted his hands in disgust and stomped off to the locker room.

"Tiny!" Diana called out. "Come on!" But her brother kept walking. She shook her head. Why was

Tiny acting like a fool about this? "Fuck. So now he hates me."

"Lesson one," Hector said sharply. "No personal business in the gym." Then his tone softened. "Use my office to change clothes while I figure out where to put you."

After Diana exchanged her baggy jeans for baggy shorts she examined the boxing photos on Hector's wall. As she left Hector's office she noticed a yellowed sign above the door: Boxing Is Brains Over Brawn.

If that's true I'm finished, Diana thought as she left the office. At the moment she was too nervous to think straight.

Hector proved to be a patient teacher and started her out slowly. First he led Diana to a mirror and showed her the basic stance: Hands in loose fists in front of the jaw, left foot forward, knees springy and relaxed. Diana was a good student. She watched Hector carefully, then studied her reflection in the mirror.

The stance came naturally to her, Hector noted. He moved on to the basic jab. He stood in front of a nearby heavy bag and snapped out his left arm, the fist twisting on impact. He repeated the jab a few times, then told Diana to try it.

Again, it didn't take her long to find a rhythm. Hector stood beside her making tiny corrections. "Snap, snap—" He pulled his fist back. "Springs back to you."

Hector demonstrated the basic right punch. "Same as your jab—different footwork."

Diana swung a hard right, throwing her body forward. Hector lightly pushed her shoulder, and she stumbled. He grabbed her and pulled her upright.

"No balance that way," Hector told her. "Look at me."

Diana watched intently as Hector glided left to right, forward and back, smooth and light as a dancer. His moves seemed to radiate from an unbroken center. *Looks easy enough,* Diana speculated. She was wrong.

Hector's skill made the move seem easy, but when Diana tried, she shuffled awkwardly, totally off balance. Hector took her shoulders and moved her around step by step. Then he stepped back, and she tried on her own.

Dozens of times he stopped her; correcting her posture, her footwork, her balance, until finally she learned how to circle, jab, jab, punch—circle, jab, jab, punch. . . . Hector didn't show it, but he was mildly impressed by the kid's intensity.

"Let's move over to the speedbag," the trainer announced, satisfied Diana had grasped the basic moves. He lifted his fists and lightly battered the leather bag in a slow, steady rhythm.

Hector paused and waved her over. "You try it."

Diana stepped up and began hitting the small bag, trying to keep a rhythm, but the bag kept bouncing away from her fists.

Hector walked away. Practice would take care of the small bag. She needed to work it out on her own. "Soon you won't think while you do this," he predicted, spinning his fists. "You'll daydream."

Diana kept trying, but after two punches she lost the rhythm. In frustration she began smacking the small bag hard with her right, trying to knock it off the hook.

"Guess you're ready for the big time," Hector observed when he returned. He led her to one of the heavy bags. "Try something your own size."

Hector held the bag steady while Diana flicked her jab, twisting her fists on impact. The trainer could feel her natural power, but she was clumsy. "Move, move around the bag," he urged. "Nothing stays still in the boxing ring."

Diana tried to take his advice, but one foot crossed

over the other. Hector pushed the bag into her, and she fell back. Hector mimicked her, crossing his feet and stumbling like a drunk. She didn't laugh.

"Okay, let's try some endurance work. You probably know how to use this." He handed her a jump rope.

Diana used to be pretty good, but she was out of practice—and tired. Sweat drenched her skin, and her arms felt heavy and stiff. Finally she got going, but in a minute or so she was nearly exhausted. She stopped to catch her breath and glimpsed Adrian nearby. He, too, was skipping rope. The rope and his feet were a blur as he executed a complicated routine. Slowly, Diana started again. Another minute and she was drained. She dropped the rope, ready to pack it in.

Hector appeared at her side. "You don't stop till the bell rings," he instructed her.

Diana groaned. Another three minutes in boxing hell. As she began skipping rope, Tiny emerged from the locker room. He ignored her as he passed.

"Hey—come on," Diana called after him, but he didn't respond.

"Okay, kid," Hector announced. "You're done for today. Talk to Ira about getting a locker. He's in the office."

Bone tired, Diana walked numbly past the boxers working out on the various bags without even noticing their curious—and appreciative—stares. When she got to the office she saw Ira behind the desk, deeply engrossed in a phone conversation. He waved her inside and pointed to an empty chair.

Grateful to be sitting down, Diana waited while Ira finished his phone call. She half listened to the snatches of conversation, too tired to care what was being said. Ira was the owner of the gym and a sometime fight promoter.

"Sure, he'll make the weight—the kid's been sleeping in Saran Wrap for the past two weeks."

Diana looked at the wall, covered with yellowing photographs of boxers. She recognized some of the more famous ones from TV documentaries. Sugar Ray Robinson, Joe Louis, Rocky Marciano, and her favorite, Muhammad Ali. Most of them were posed in the standard fighter's stance, others had their fists raised in triumphant post-fight salutes. *Right now I couldn't lift my hands that high,* Diana thought, wishing Ira would get off the phone.

Ira raised his voice. "Hey, whose idea was it to keep him at junior lightweight anyway? Exactly.

Don't get bent outta shape over this. Saturday he'll be at twenty-nine. Yeah, okay—talk to you later."

The burly gym owner hung up the phone, then turned and squinted at Diana. "You're the girl Hector told me about. And you need a locker."

Diana nodded. "Yeah."

Stiffly, Ira came around his desk and took a ring of keys from a nail on the wall. He motioned for Diana to follow and shambled to the door. "We ain't big-time, hon," he rumbled amiably. "We're not really set up for the ladies yet. Neighborhoods like this one don't catch on quick with the lawyer types."

Ira went to a door near the entrance and opened it. He stepped inside and pulled a string hanging from a light bulb in the ceiling. Diana saw they were in a large supply closet filled with old brooms and pails and an industrial sink in one corner. Ira kicked the brooms aside and handed Diana the keys. "We don't use this anymore," he told her. "It's yours if you wanna throw your stuff somewhere."

"Thanks," Diana said. She closed the door and wearily shuffled to the stairs.

The trip home seemed to take hours. Every muscle in Diana's body seemed wrung out like wet laundry. The worst part was, she had to fix dinner for the family when she finally arrived home. She barely managed to make it through by cooking spaghetti, the easiest meal she knew.

As usual, nobody talked much, but Diana could feel her brother's tension across the dinner table. From time to time their eyes met, but Tiny said nothing. Exhausted, she went right to bed after dinner. Diana was asleep even before her head hit the pillow.

Chapter 4

Mr. Coolidge could have used a lesson in public speaking. He went on in a steady drone about the nature of mass and ions while the entire class stared into space.

Marisol folded a note and pushed it across the aisle with her foot. Diana seemed to be watching the teacher, then leaned over and picked up the note.

Diana read the note: "Fulton Mall after detention?" She glanced at Marisol and shook her head no.

"Why?" Marisol mouthed silently.

Diana shrugged and silently answered, "I can't."

"Girls," Mr. Coolidge called out, peering over his glasses. "You both know how this works."

Both Diana and Marisol sank down in their seats.

"Yes, Mr. Coolidge," they chimed in unison. They both thought the teacher was kind of cute, in a dorky way.

After class, Diana used her detention time to study, since her usual study hours were being taken up by her training. She spotted Marisol outside the window, making an *F* and *M* with her fingers, for *Fulton Mall*. Diana shook her head and pointed to her book as if she had to go home and study.

The detention bell finally rang. Diana made sure Marisol wasn't still around, then hurried off the school grounds to catch the subway.

When Diana arrived at the gym, Hector wrapped her hands with cloth strips. He applied the wraps with almost loving care, then put tape over her knuckles and between her fingers. Diana was impressed with how quickly and neatly he taped her left hand. He immediately started on her right.

"Watch me do this, 'cause soon you'll have to do it yourself," Hector told her. "Make a fist."

Diana clenched her fist. "Feels good."

Next Hector put her hands into small black boxing gloves. Then he slipped his hands into a pair of padded mitts. When the start bell sounded, Hector held up the mitts for Diana to jab as he rapidly shouted instructions. "Jab twice. Now jab and right. Hook, hook . . ."

Breathlessly, Diana followed directions until the red light signaled the end of the round.

"Here's how you hook," Hector said, crouching to demonstrate a left hook. Awkwardly Diana tried to imitate him. Hector repeated, this time in slow motion.

"Keep it simple. Don't waste no energy," he said, hooking again with powerful ease.

The bell sounded. "Okay, hook!" Hector commanded.

Diana went to work. She crouched and hooked, this time with swift explosiveness. Even Hector seemed surprised.

"Not bad," he said, moving around her. "Now jab, jab, *right* . . ." Before the round ended, Diana had learned seven combinations on the mitts.

"Don't drag your feet," Hector scolded.

Diana couldn't help it. She was still worn out from the previous workout, but she noticed that the muscle stiffness was gone. The bell sounded. She shook out her arms and legs and started again.

Hector liked what he saw. The kid worked hard, didn't complain and picked up fast. She was still raw, but she threw punches hard and fast. There was an animal grace to her body in motion.

"Okay, time," Hector called, pulling off the mitts. "Move to the speedbag."

Diana started hitting the small leather bag but couldn't find a rhythm. Frustrated, she stepped back and saw Tiny starting on the speedbag next to hers. Her brother pretended she wasn't there.

Diana dropped her hands. "Tiny—how long's this gonna last?"

Tiny kept battering the speedbag as if he didn't hear. But he was as bad as Diana. He paused and looked at her. "I don't know what you're talking about."

Diana strutted closer, mocking Tiny's macho indifference. "I don't know what you're talking about," she said in a deep, moronic voice. She playfully tapped her brother on the head. "Stop being such a tough guy."

She went back to the speedbag without much success. Tiny watched her, still unable to figure it out. "Why you gotta do this, huh?" Tiny blurted finally. "You can't *pay* for it."

"Whadda you care?" she countered, struggling with the bag.

"You should tell Dad."

"Are you for real? This would drive him nuts. So keep your mouth shut."

Tiny stared at her. "I can't believe you sometimes."

Unable to handle the speedbag, Diana walked away in midround. She was totally frustrated by her inability to master it.

"Hey!" Hector called out. "You still got two rounds."

Diana glared at him stubbornly. "I can't do it right."

"Then get back over there till you can."

"But it's pissing me off."

Hector was working with another young fighter, but he stopped and came closer. "You think this stuff is gonna happen overnight? Think it just came natural to these guys? Gonna come natural to you?" he mocked harshly. "Huh?"

"No," Diana murmured, head down.

Hector softened his tone. "This time, work the bag slow and steady, and don't stop till the red light goes on."

Head still down, Diana remained where she was. She struggled to control her emotions. *Get over it,* she told herself. *You can't walk out.* Slowly, she moved back to the speedbag.

The next day, as Diana left her classroom after the last bell, her entire body felt stiff. She moved gingerly through the flow of students to her locker area.

She spotted Marisol, but coming closer, Diana noticed Veronica standing with her.

Veronica nudged Marisol. "Look. Your bodyguard," she said, loud enough for Diana to hear.

Fuming at Marisol's betrayal, Diana scowled at Veronica. "The slave girls get a day off when you slum it with Marisol?"

Veronica lost her cool. "I've had it with your dismal crap. You're sick, you hear me? You don't even know me."

"I know all I have to," Diana spat. She gave Veronica a shove for good measure.

"Quit it," Marisol warned, stepping between them.

"She just hangs out with you to get to me!" Diana blurted.

Marisol shook her head. "You should know, you're the center of the universe, right?"

"It's the truth," Diana insisted.

The bell rang, and Marisol turned to Veronica. "We're gonna be late. Later, Diana."

Marisol turned and walked away. Veronica gave Diana a superior smile, then joined Marisol. Still fuming with hurt and indignation, Diana watched them leave.

"You said you'd do my braids," she called to Marisol.

Marisol kept walking. "Phone me when there's an opening in your busy schedule." She and Veronica disappeared into the crowd before Diana could answer.

Diana was learning that her sore muscles loosened up after a few minutes of shadowboxing in the ring. Maybe that was why Hector waited before entering the ring with his leather mitts.

"Okay, jab, jab, right . . ." the trainer intoned.

Diana focused as they went through the seven combinations. She imagined the mitt was Veronica and blasted a left hook. Then a jab, jab, right . . . all with tremendous fury.

"Hold it." Hector dropped the mitts. "Too much power. Just box for now."

They began again. Diana snapped another hard right.

Hector stepped back. "You deaf? I said too much power." He motioned for her to repeat the jab, right hook. The combination flew past his jaw as Diana executed the moves with dazzling speed. "You've been working on your hook," he congratulated her. "Finish with your uppercut."

This time Diana was too eager. She repeated the combination, but her wild uppercut almost came back to hit her own face.

Hector stifled a laugh. "All force, no technique."

Diana felt her face flush with embarrassment. "Come on, keep going," she told Hector. "Round's not over."

Hector bobbed around her, mitts high. Diana threw hard punches, but half didn't connect, and she tired out before the bell sounded.

"Hey, power's only half the story," Hector urged. "You scared of me? Huh?"

"No—I'm not scared."

"Here I am," Hector told her. "I want to get you on the ropes so I can dance on your face."

To demonstrate, he came at her quickly, his moves threatening, forcing her back against the ropes. Confused, Diana lifted her mitts to protect her face as Hector hovered around her, tapping her at will. Everywhere she turned he was there. She seemed locked in his space.

He threw a few speedy combinations, and she tried to duck around them.

"You look powerless in front of me," Hector said, backing away. He rushed her again, but this time Diana instinctively shuffled to the side and turned. Hector stopped at the ropes and smiled. "Ahhh," he congratulated her. "Someone wants you where you don't wanna be—just get outta their way."

Hector half-turned. "Look here." He turned again, demonstrating a tight, precise swivel on the balls of his feet. "Keep the footwork smaller. And you got another opening to throw some punches. Here—come at me."

Diana moved swiftly, but Hector stepped, turned, and was at her side—able to hook her from a new angle.

Diana nodded and waved Hector on. When he attacked she smoothly stepped and turned.

"Yes!" Hector beamed at her. "*Now* we're boxing!"

Diana smiled, panting with exhaustion. Just then Adrian walked past, wearing his headgear and gloves. He smiled back at her. It was a perfect moment.

The next moment wasn't so good. Hector insisted she do three sets of sit-ups to end the session. He stood there and counted off each set of twenty. By the second set Diana was breathing very hard. Only sheer pride pushed her to keep going.

"You should start roadwork," Hector told her solemnly. "Run three miles four times a week."

"Three miles?" It sounded like three hundred to Diana. "You got to be kidding."

"At *least* three. This rate, you couldn't last one round in the ring." Hector started counting off Diana's final set.

"But I got power," Diana grunted. "You said so."

"Big deal—you got the endurance of a corpse." He walked away and sat on a nearby bench while she painfully completed her last two sit-ups. Diana rolled off the slant board and joined him on the bench.

Hector offered her a squirt of water from his bottle. She took it gratefully, then stared ahead, breathing deeply. After a few moments she glanced at him.

"I'll use the track at school."

"Don't worry about clocking yourself yet," he advised with a satisfied nod.

Diana gave him a weary look. Then her gaze wandered to the far ring, where Adrian and Ray were preparing to spar. Don the trainer laced up Ray's gloves while Adrian's trainer, Cal, did the same for him.

Then Diana saw a shapely young woman in a tight dress cruising toward the ring. Heads turned as she made her way through the gym.

"So, who are the greatest fighters?" Diana asked, turning back to Hector.

"The greatest?" Hector paused. "That's a real long list." He leaned back, thinking. "There's Sugar Ray Robinson—some say it never got better than him. There's always Ali. There's Roberto Duran, Joe Louis, Willie Pep. There's Griffith, Hagler, Frazier. Alexis Arguello. Sandy Saddler. . . . The greatest? It's all a matter of taste. I prefer the lightweights."

"How come?"

Hector's voice dropped, as if conferring a secret. "The lower weight divisions demand speed *and* power. And grace. Sometimes I watch the bigger guys fight and I think they're clumsy, like animals." He snorted in disgust. "Heavyweights . . . the big pros . . . it's all about the purse."

Hector shook his head. "But that's what the people want. They wanna see that one guy be heavy-weight champion of the world, driving nice cars, eating steaks, pretty lady on his arm—then he gets fat and clobbered next time he fights."

They both watched Adrian and Ray sparring in the ring. Adrian was the better boxer—quick-footed, agile, graceful, smartly defensive. Ray had power and raw instinct but he lost his focus easily.

Diana kept her eyes on the ring. "Were you ever a fighter?"

"Oh, sure," Hector said casually. "In Panama. I had my day once."

"What happened?"

Hector shrugged. "What happens to most of us who do it? We lose. We get tired." He kept watching Adrian. "I see a fighter from the outside. I show a fighter how to beat the opponent at his own game. This I know about boxing."

He turned to face Diana and tapped his chest. "But on the inside. *Here*. I was never a fighter."

Diana didn't quite know what he meant, but it felt deep. She felt as if something important had been revealed to her.

"There's only two of you in that ring," Hector

went on, watching Adrian and Ray go at it. "The sport doesn't choose many players."

Diana hesitated. "Then most of these guys here—what are they, just dreaming?"

"Sure they are," Hector said flatly. "They got no choice! Some of 'em—this is what they live for . . . this is their whole life."

"Was it like that for you?"

Hector squinted as if trying to recall. "To fight? Aww—looking back, probably not. I didn't have what it takes."

"What's it take?" Diana asked intently. "To be great, I mean."

Hector kept watching the two young fighters in the ring. "I don't know," he said slowly. "A real strong will."

The final bell sounded. Adrian and Ray moved to separate corners. Diana's stomach clenched when she saw the shapely girl in the tight dress at ringside. The girl couldn't keep her eyes off Adrian as she edged toward his corner.

Adrian noticed her and raised his glove. The girl waved back. Diana felt like throwing up.

"I was gonna go to a fight at the Forum next week," Hector said. "If you wanna see some good lightweight action, Ira gets discount tickets some-times."

Still distracted by the scene at ringside, Diana didn't register the comment right away. Finally it dawned that Hector was extending an invitation. She blinked at him, somewhat surprised. "I can come with you?"

Hector shrugged. "It's no big thing."

But it was for Diana. "For real?"

"Maybe you'll learn something."

Diana nodded. She already had. "Yeah. Oh—here." She handed Hector some cash. He pocketed it with a nod.

Diana gathered her things. She started to leave, then paused. "Hector . . ."

The trainer looked up.

"Thanks," Diana said.

Hector smiled and turned his attention to the ring.

Diana left the gym with a new sense of herself. For the first time in her life an adult male had treated her as an equal—and with respect.

Chapter 5

"I hope you've all completed the assigned reading and finished the worksheets," Mr. Price told the class. Then he launched into one of his droning lectures. "Today we're going to learn about a fundamental concept in science—the second law of thermodynamics. The primary element in this law is heat."

Mr. Price checked to see that the students were listening before he continued. "What is heat, anyway? A simple definition is this: heat is the energy possessed by molecules because of their motion."

The students quietly took notes. Diana tried to concentrate, but her mind was in the gym, working combinations.

Later that afternoon she went outside to the

beat-up track behind the school. Stiffly, she began jogging around the cinder oval. Diana had heard it was four laps to a mile. That meant she had to do twelve laps before going to the gym.

At first it felt good to run. As Diana's muscles warmed up, the words of the teacher's lecture came back to her. But by the fourth lap Diana was about to puke. She walked unsteadily to the wire fence and leaned against it for support. Her face and hair were drenched with sweat, and her legs felt like spaghetti.

Hector's right about my endurance, Diana thought. She pushed herself away from the fence and slowly began to jog one more lap. Her workout attracted a few stray students who hung around to watch and make rude remarks.

Diana paid no attention to the hecklers as she slowly circled the track, her mind focused on completing the last torturous lap. She had always been strong-willed, but boxing tested her to the limit.

"Yo, is your momma chasin' ya?"

Diana heard that one, and it sparked her pent-up resentment. Immediately she veered off the track toward the source of the catcall. He was a young guy with twin gold earrings, and he seemed totally unprepared for her reaction. He backed a half-step away from the fence as Diana approached.

"What'd you say about my mother?" she demanded, bristling for a fight.

He lifted his arms and smiled. "Chill, Sugar Ray, just playin'."

In the corner of her eye Diana glimpsed two other guys approaching. Their menacing gait hinted that things could get ugly. Street smarts prevailed over Diana's temper. She turned and jogged across the field to the safety of the school building. *It's different in the gym,* she reflected, chest heaving with effort. *Nobody there disses me.*

The Brooklyn Athletic Club had become a safe haven for Diana. Someplace where she could be herself, by herself, following her own dream. She really didn't think about becoming a professional. It was the challenge that kept her coming back night after night.

But this night Diana wasn't doing that well. Her legs were stiff from jogging, and her feet felt heavy. Hector was coming at her with the big mitts, crowding her off balance. Diana tried a combination, but Hector tagged her. Frustrated, Diana swung wildly at him.

"What's this?" Hector held up his arms in disappointment. "You call this boxing?" He began to shuffle, swinging his arms like an ape. Then he jerked his legs, mocking her footwork. "And you dance too much."

Diana lowered her head. More than anyone, she didn't want to disappoint Hector.

"Keep your eyes on me—not my hands," the trainer told her. "That's how you give yourself away."

Hector lifted the mitts again and Diana threw a jab. The trainer stopped.

"Your elbows fly up." He lifted her arm so her elbow was parallel to the ground. "Now watch." Hector faked an uppercut, driving Diana back.

"Look how open you leave yourself," Hector scolded. "You're boxing *with* someone—*they* wanna get in your space. Keep it contained."

Diana gave him two clean jabs and a crisp right hook.

"Better," Hector encouraged. "One more time."

The final bell rang, and Hector walked away, waving at Cal and Adrian as he passed. Adrian nodded at Hector, then looked back at Diana. Taken off guard, Diana turned aside. But she was secretly pleased he had glanced her way.

Later she put in her time with the jump rope.

She was doing it easily now, feet moving lightly in rhythm. Once in a while she would try one of the faster tricks. Her breathing came smoothly, and her body felt stronger.

A dark shape rushed at her. Instinctively she jumped back, still jumping rope.

Hector grinned. "Just testing those reflexes."

The trainer was impressed when he saw Diana working the speedbag. She was steadier and more focused, picking up a propulsive beat as she hit the bag faster. Hector nodded approval.

"Friday you spar," he announced.

Diana continued to pound the bag. "I'm ready to?"

Hector smiled. "You're a quick study."

"I am?" She felt as if he'd just awarded her a medal.

Hector brought her back to earth. "You gotta pay me for last week."

Her concentration crumbled and the bag flapped sideways. She tried to pick up the rhythm again but her focus was gone.

All the way home, Diana tried to figure out some way to raise money. Stealing from her father was out. She still felt bad about the last time. *There was one option,* Diana thought, but she hated to use it.

* * *

Ruby's Pawn Shop was two blocks away from the projects, right next to the liquor store. Once her father had sent her down to Ruby's to pawn his watch. He'd been too embarrassed to go himself.

A few weeks later Sandro had given Diana some cash and sent her to redeem the watch. Diana had learned a little from these transactions. When she entered the shop, Big Al, the proprietor, stood behind the bulletproof glass, examining a bracelet.

Diana went up to the glass and pushed a silver object through the opening. "What can you give me for this?"

It was a silver locket—one of the few things Diana had that had belonged to her mother. Big Al examined the piece.

"It's real silver," Diana prompted.

The pawnbroker opened it. Inside were two faded photographs: her mother and her father, both young. "I can't sell it with the pictures," Big Al grumbled. He pushed the locket through the opening. "Strangers to everyone but you."

"Yeah." Diana carefully extracted the small photographs and put them into her pocket.

"I'll give you forty bucks for it."

Diana acted surprised. "That's all?"

"It's not worth more than that," Big Al said flatly.

Diana pushed the locket through the opening. "Sixty."

Big Al pushed it back. "Gimme a break."

"Please."

Big Al heaved a reluctant sigh. "Fifty bucks. Final offer."

Diana hesitated. "Guess I'll take it." She touched the locket one last time, then pushed it through the slot in the bulletproof glass.

Outside in the sunshine, Diana looked at the bleached photographs of her parents. *Strangers to me, too,* she thought. She put the photos away and headed for the bus stop.

It felt good to be back in the gym, but Diana was nervous. This would be her first time in the ring with a sparring partner. People would be watching. *Please don't let me blow it,* Diana prayed. She warmed up carefully before climbing into the ring where Hector was waiting.

As she neared, Diana saw her sparring partner. Her belly clenched. It was Ray, the guy she'd hit that first day. *Why him?* She silently asked Hector.

Hector didn't say anything as he laced up her

gloves and then adjusted her headgear. "Too tight?" he asked, pulling the strap.

Diana nodded. "It's okay." She glanced across the ring, where Don stood lacing Ray's gloves. "You think this is a good idea?"

"Ray knows, no funny stuff," Hector assured her. "Just keep it relaxed. No pressure."

Just then Ray looked across the ring and gave Diana a nasty smirk.

Don shook his head. "Try an' be a gentleman."

"Take it easy on me this time, okay?" Ray jeered at Diana.

"Don't be a dick and I'll try." Diana turned to Hector. "Why'd he have to say that?"

Hector grabbed her shoulders *"Ignore him! Here—"* He put her mouthpiece in place and slipped through the ropes. She was alone.

Adrian's trainer, Cal, joined Hector and Don on the ring apron. Tiny and a few other fighters straggled over to watch.

"How's it working with her?" Cal muttered.

Hector kept his eyes on Diana. "Gotta pay the bills."

"When you're that desperate, borrow from me."

Hector gave Cal a bored smile. *You're about to*

swallow that insult, he thought. *The kid's a natural.*

The bell rang, and Diana's first round of sparring began.

Both she and Ray advanced to the center of the ring and touched gloves. Then they started circling. Ray threw a few halfhearted jabs, but both of them were tight. Diana felt awkward at first, but Ray wasn't doing much better as he circled her, pawing jabs. Instinctively, Diana countered with a hard right that made contact with Ray's head.

Diana froze. "Sorry!" she mumbled through the mouthpiece.

"Aw, come on," Hector shouted. "You're not sorry. Don't ever be sorry!"

Unsettled, Diana glanced nervously at Hector and Tiny, wishing she were somewhere else. Then she saw Ray moving in and she focused. She tentatively threw a jab, then another.

Suddenly Ray smacked her with a left hook. It felt like a lightbulb exploding in her face. An alarm went off in Diana's head. As if she'd just woken up, Diana began moving around Ray with more precision.

Three minutes is a long time in the ring. Diana snapped a nice jab to Ray's ear, and ducked away from another hook. But he tagged her with a few of his own jabs as they continued to circle each other. When the bell rang neither of them had really done much, but Diana was satisfied. She'd gotten through it without making a fool of herself.

Sweating profusely and breathing hard, Diana went to her corner where Hector was waiting. He squirted water into her dry mouth.

"When your jab makes contact, don't give him time to recover," Hector instructed her. "Rush him with some of those combinations we been doing."

Diana hung her head. "It's like I forgot everything you been teaching me."

Hector leaned closer. "Don't think so much. You're doing good."

The sparring match was only two rounds, but when the bell rang, Diana wasn't sure she could last another three minutes.

Diana circled and jabbed, trying to keep Ray outside. The strategy worked. Every time Ray would try to move in, she used her hook. Once or twice Ray hit her in the body, but she slipped most of his punches. Near the closing seconds Diana noticed Ray seemed wiped out.

When the bell rang, Ray touched her gloves. "But you too pretty to be a killer."

Exhausted, Diana ignored him. She turned to Hector, who removed her headgear. "Next time he'll wanna crush you," the trainer warned.

Later, when Diana came out of the supply closet she used as a locker room, she found Hector waiting for her.

"You did good tonight," the trainer said as he walked out with her.

A warm glow of elation eased Diana's body aches. She had held her own against an experienced male fighter. As they left the building she saw Adrian unlocking his car. Uncertainty cut through her elation. She wasn't an experienced flirt like that other girl.

Hector paused near Adrian's car. "You've been working hard."

Adrian nodded. "Yeah. Guess so."

"Cal's got you conditioned real good."

"Thanks."

Diana edged away. "Later, Hector."

"Oh yeah, see ya. How you getting home?"

Diana paused. "The 61. Or the F. I'm in Red Hook."

"I'm driving that way," Adrian said.

A bolt of panic shot though Diana. "I don't mind the bus."

"This place is deserted at night," Hector reminded her.

"I'll be fine," Diana said lamely.

"Okay, but it's no trouble," Adrian assured her. "I'm just in Gowanus."

"Oh, all right," Diana said casually. But her heart was racing.

Hector got into his car. "Bye, guys." He was smiling to himself as he started the motor and eased away, leaving the two of them alone.

Diana and Adrian rode in silence for a while through the deserted streets. Diana was slightly uncomfortable, and dead tired. She wondered if Adrian had seen her spar with Ray.

"The F and G are my nightmare trains," Adrian said, staring through the windshield.

"The G is the worst," Diana agreed.

"No wonder people move outta Queens."

"You're lucky to have wheels."

Adrian shrugged. "Lucky's winning the lottery. My dad, he's a mechanic, has me run errands all day—all over Brooklyn—for this ride. Always gotta be thinkin' *expansion*." Abruptly he stopped and looked away, as if he

73

had said too much. "Anyway. You in high school?"

Diana nodded. "My last year, I hope. Still in school?"

"Am I immature or something?"

"No," Diana said quickly, somewhat embarrassed. "I just thought . . ."

Adrian gave her a big smile. "I'm just playing with you. I graduated last year. My only achievement in life."

"Yeah, right." Diana furtively glanced at him. She liked his smile.

"It's true. My mom cried when I got my diploma."

His mom, Diana thought wistfully. She tried to imagine the scene.

"That's nice," she murmured.

Adrian fell silent as if he was trying to remember. Every once in a while Diana would catch a glimpse of him, intent over the steering wheel. He had nice eyes and a strong, honest face.

As they neared the projects they passed a string of street-corner bodegas. Packs of kids hung out in the neon glow, playfully pushing and shoving each other. The same scene repeated itself from corner to corner until they finally arrived at Diana's block.

"You gotta tell me where to turn," Adrian said softly.

"Oh." Diana peered through the windshield. She pointed to the main entrance. "Right in here. Then a left."

Adrian slowly drove along the narrow road that curved through the sprawling housing project. He stopped in front of the huge glass doors of Diana's building. "This it?"

She nodded, uncertain of what to say.

"What floor you on?"

"The eleventh."

"You're up there." Adrian peered up through the windshield as if he could see into her apartment.

"Yeah." They both smiled at each other. For some reason it made Diana feel good that he cared what floor she lived on. She opened the car door. "Thanks for the ride."

Adrian gunned the motor. "Be seeing you."

Diana ran up the stairs into the lobby. She turned to watch the red taillights of Adrian's car fade from sight.

Dinner was over when Diana entered the apartment. Her father was at the sink, washing dishes, while Tiny sat at the table doing homework. There was still a place at the table set for Diana.

She went to the table and started to eat. Tiny gave her a warning glance across the table. Diana looked up and saw her father standing with his arms crossed, staring at her. He used to look at her mother the same way.

"What?" Diana said finally.

"You're late."

"I was hanging out with Marisol." She avoided looking at her brother.

"You can thank Tiny for dinner."

Nobody thanks me when I cook dinner most every night, Diana thought. But she was hungry and grateful for the food. "Thanks, bro," she said dutifully.

Tiny kept his head lowered, trying to stay out of the tension between Diana and their father. Diana ate in silence, but she could feel Sandro watching her.

Diana's father turned to leave the kitchen. "Take a shower after dinner—you stink."

She grinned and lifted one arm to sniff her armpit. "Huh," she said as if surprised. "You're right. I think I will take one."

The long, hot shower was exactly what her body needed after the sparring match with Ray. She was beginning to ache in places he had tagged her. Afterward she felt refreshed. She lay on her bed and stared at the ceiling, thinking about Adrian. He was very gentle for a fighter.

The door opened and Tiny slipped in. "Pop thinks you're dogging some guy," he confided.

She sat up. "Huh—that's typical."

Tiny hesitated. "You looked all right in there with Ray."

"He was taking it easy on me."

"No. He was afraid," Tiny said with a trace of pride.

Diana understood her brother had finally accepted her as a boxer. It made her feel closer to him. "It's way more tiring than it looks, huh?"

Tiny stared out the window. "What's he after anyway—making me fight?" He looked at Diana and shook his head helplessly. "I just wanna make him happy."

Diana knew what he was trying to say. Tiny would rather be taking art lessons. But she also knew there was no pleasing their father, either way. "Yeah, well—good luck to you." She sighed.

Chapter 6

Diana had a new jogging routine. She got up at dawn and went out into the streets. Her route took her through a deserted industrial neighborhood to a housing project about two miles from hers.

She paused at the entrance to a trio of huge buildings and leaned on her knees, breathing hard. In front of her was a large sign that read: Gowanus Community Houses—Building Today for a Better Tomorrow.

Adrian lived in one of the buildings. Diana wasn't sure exactly which one. She turned and started jogging toward home. If she made it back in time she could take a shower before she went off to school.

Her father had already left for work when she got back. Tiny was still asleep. Diana showered quickly and hastily prepared breakfast: cereal, banana, and milk. Hector had been lecturing her about proper nutrition. She put a bowl of cereal next to the milk carton for Tiny. Her brother was always late in the morning.

It used to take her twenty minutes to walk to school, but since she had started training it took about ten. She was pleased to find she had some time before her first class. She dumped her gear into her locker and headed for the library to cram for an upcoming test.

Marisol was in Diana's social studies class. When the bell rang, Diana headed for her locker with Marisol close behind.

"How can the history of the world be so fucking boring?" Diana complained as Marisol caught up to her.

"And all those people are dead, too," Marisol agreed.

Diana didn't answer. She just kept walking.

"You holding a grudge against me cuz of that dumb thing with Veronica?" Marisol demanded finally. "If you are, I gotta say it makes me—"

Diana turned. "*You* were holding a grudge against *me.*"

"I was pissed at you for stirring up shit," Marisol corrected her.

Diana heaved a sigh. "Okay. I was an idiot. I can't tell you who to hang with. Even if they are lame." She started walking again.

Marisol was surprised by Diana's new attitude, but she was still curious. She was certain Diana had a secret boyfriend. She broke into a gentle trot to catch up to Diana again.

"I wanna hang with you and you never wanna do anything with me!" Marisol called after Diana. "Seems you always got places to go."

Diana stopped at her locker.

"You gonna deny something's going on?" Marisol prodded.

"You're gonna laugh," Diana said as she threw her social studies books into her locker.

"What?" Marisol was bouncing with curiosity now. Her long curls were bobbing up and down.

"You're gonna think I'm full of shit."

"It's a guy—" Marisol squealed.

"*No.* I mean—"

"He's here at school?" Marisol leaned in closer, waiting for Diana to confide in her.

"No, no—it's not a guy."

"Then *what?*"

Diana took a deep breath. "I'm training to be a boxer," she said casually.

"Oh, be serious," Marisol scolded.

"I am serious. I work with Hector Soto at the Brooklyn Athletic Club on Front Street."

Marisol blinked. She started throwing mock punches. "You mean pow-wow-wow?" She paused for a moment, taking in the news. "Huh—that's cool. You get hit?"

Diana smiled and nodded.

"In the face?"

"It happens." They started walking to their next class.

"You fight guys?" Marisol asked, fascinated.

"That's all there is over there—"

"You got guys hitting you in the face?" Marisol repeated.

Diana stopped. "This is for real, Marisol," she said carefully. "You're all alone in there. Like you're all you got." She looked away and shook her head. "Can't explain it exactly."

Marisol had never seen Diana so intent on anything before. She was different somehow. "You are crazy. My crazy friend."

81

"It's fun is all—"

"Doesn't sound like fun to me."

Diana couldn't resist mentioning the rest. "And there's this one guy—"

"I knew it," Marisol squealed, yanking Diana's arm.

"Damn! He's light on his feet," Diana said with a faraway smile.

"Name?" Marisol asked, all business now.

"Adrian."

"What kinda girly name is that?"

"Hey!" Diana warned. "He's one hundred percent—know what I mean?"

Both of them started to laugh. Marisol gave Diana a long, knowing look.

"And how would you know this percentage?"

"Guesswork, Marisol," Diana said sharply. "How come everything's gotta be a romance with you?"

"What can I say?" Marisol said sweetly. "I live for that shit. Anyway, I was right in the first place, wasn't I?"

Diana heaved an exasperated sigh. "Forget I mentioned it."

"Oh? That Miss Stone Cold's got a crush? I don't think so."

Diana whirled, but Marisol had turned and was

being swallowed up by the tide of kids rushing to class. *Too late now*, Diana thought ruefully. *Marisol's like CNN*. Before lunch everybody, including Veronica, would have the news.

The Felt Forum at Penn Plaza in Manhattan was the real deal.

A neon sign in front announced: Friday Fights at the Forum. Fans streamed in to watch professional boxers defend their titles or become new champions. The air was charged with excitement as Diana followed Hector inside.

Diana felt slightly awed by the sight of the arena. The boxing ring sat in the center of a large auditorium lit from above by rows of tiny fluorescent lights. To Diana it seemed like some grand ballroom in the movies—and the big dance was in the center ring.

Military rows of folding chairs covered the smooth floor. Hector led Diana to a section where some of his friends were seated. Diana watched in fascination as the arena filled up. Whole families, couples, men swaggering and laughing, single guys sipping beer from bottles hidden in paper bags under their coats; the Forum was buzzing in three or four languages.

Hector's friends were a mixed bunch: Raul was a

lawyer, Beni was a paramedic, and Gordo was an ex-fighter. Like Diana's father, they were from Panama. Diana understood little of what they said but enough to know they were talking about her.

Raul glanced at her, then at Hector with raised eyebrows. Hector said something in rapid Spanish that made Beni laugh. From the look on Raul's face, Diana knew Hector had straightened him out.

Scanning the crowd, Diana spotted a tall man wearing a full-length fur coat, walking through the crowd as if he were the king.

"Piece of work, right?"

Diana turned. Hector had noticed her staring.

"Who is he?" she asked.

Hector snorted in disapproval. "Dante Prince, he calls himself—big-time promoter. Always got new meat to peddle." He half-stood and waved at someone.

Diana's stomach fluttered when she saw it was Adrian. He was coming down the aisle looking for an empty seat.

"Adrian!" Hector called.

Diana wished he hadn't. Adrian smiled faintly at them. Diana looked away.

"Come and sit with us," Hector called above the noise.

Adrian lifted his hands. "No seats."

"Raul, Beni—move over," Hector said in Spanish.

"That's okay, I see some," Adrian said, pointing to the back.

Hector and Diana watched Adrian make his way to a bank of empty seats. Diana was both relieved and disappointed.

"He doesn't feel social," Hector said absently. "I understand."

Diana didn't really understand. Adrian stirred feelings in her she never knew she had. And she didn't know if she wanted them.

Just then the announcer entered the ring. The audience turned its attention to the fight. Two boxers entered the ring for a three-round match. The announcer called out their records. A referee chanted the rules, and the men touched gloves.

The bell rang and the two boxers began to circle. Having practiced the same basic moves and combinations, Diana could see how good the two young fighters really were. She was close enough to see sweat spray when their bodies collided. A bloody red blotch appeared on one fighter's nose.

Between rounds heavily made-up young women in scanty outfits and high heels held up scorecards, while the trainers rubbed down their fighters. The boxers lifted their faces to be greased or stitched by their cornermen, who shouted hard words of encouragement. Then the bell rang and the crowd noises swelled.

Diana glanced behind her and saw Adrian intently watching the fight as if trying to learn. For the rest of the night Diana did the same, studying each fighter—and fight—as the program progressed to the main event. Every so often Hector would point out some detail of a fighter's technique.

Fascinated, Diana took it all in. She could see how much better some pros were compared to the boxers who trained at her gym—and how bad some of their opponents were.

After the fights were over, many of the fans stayed in their seats. Hector and his pals noisily recounted the night's most exciting moments. Everyone seemed energized, including Diana. She saw Adrian coming down the aisle to join them.

He took a seat next to her and said, "So you're becoming a serious fan."

Diana nodded. "I liked that guy Lopez."

Hector cut in. "Garcia came back strong tonight."

Adrian gave him a knowing wink. "If my payday was as sweet as his, I'd come out fighting, too."

"Hector, I'm starved," Diana said. "Let's go eat."

"Can't. Got a date with my wife tonight," Hector said apologetically. He turned back to his pals.

Diana glanced at Adrian, who seemed ready to leave. "You hungry?" she asked impulsively.

He smiled. "I'm always hungry."

Adrian's car was being fixed, so they walked to a diner in midtown Manhattan. Diana and Adrian sat in a booth by the window, drinking sodas.

"So, give it up," Adrian said casually, his eyes on the street. "Is Hector after you?"

Suddenly Diana understood why Adrian hadn't sat with them. "Like, after my ass after me?"

"Not many girls go to fights 'less they're dragged by their boyfriends," Adrian pointed out.

"I wasn't dragged," Diana said flatly. "Neither were the chicks in the back screaming 'murder the chump.'" She grinned and shook her head. "They were out for blood, right?"

Adrian smiled. "Guess they were pretty rowdy."

Diana glanced out the window. "I wanted to see

how the pros do it." She wasn't sure he'd understand. And he didn't.

"How come you're training with Hector?"

"You mean like, at all?"

"Yeah."

Diana tried to express what boxing meant to her.
To be able to do something she was good at. To be
validated for who she was instead of put down. To
be rewarded for things she achieved on her own.
But it was too confusing.

"I do it 'cause I want to," was all she could say.

"Aren't you afraid you'll get hurt?"

"What—you're not?"

The question surprised him, and he looked away.
"No. It's just—it's a dangerous sport."

Diana shrugged. "Didn't make the cheerleading
team."

He glanced at her, slightly bewildered but curious. The waitress approached, and he intently studied the menu.

"I'll have a bacon cheeseburger. Rare," Diana
told the waitress. "And make it deluxe, with extra
bacon." She glimpsed Adrian's look and smiled. "I
said I was hungry."

"I'll have a cup of the soup and a garden salad

with Italian dressing on the side," Adrian said quietly. "That's all."

"What kind of dinner is that?" Diana asked as the waitress walked away.

"Trying to stay at my weight," Adrian told her. "I got speedy fighters in my division."

Diana was impressed. "You compete?"

"Yeah."

"And you like it?"

"Sure. Keeps me outta trouble."

"You a delinquent?"

"Not anymore," Adrian said with a touch of pride. "I got some good fights under my belt. Not much comes close to winning."

"Except for losing."

Adrian nodded and squinted out the window. Diana could tell he didn't get it, but she didn't care. She felt relaxed with him.

"Either way," he said finally. "It's hard to find your match."

Diana nodded. She watched the pedestrians strolling by, the people in Manhattan seemed different from the people in Brooklyn. "Some of those guys looked hopeless tonight."

"That's the mentality sometimes. Promoters

wanna find a fall guy to get bashed—like a public sacrifice."

Diana shook her head. "Huh, that's low. Why would you wanna fight someone weaker than you?"

" 'Cause you're gutless, that's why," Adrian answered fervently. "The whole reason for the sport is you box somebody who challenges you. What's the point of a fight that's over in a minute and a half?"

"You could say that about a lot of things."

Diana immediately regretted the remark. Adrian smiled uneasily.

"Maybe some people don't want to be challenged," Diana added.

"Yeah."

"How long have you trained?"

"Almost a year. Cal's got a whole plan mapped out for me."

Just then their food arrived. Adrian eyed Diana's heaping platter, but he wanted to tell her about his next fight. He touched her arm briefly, unaware of the gesture.

"I might be lined up against Ray in the next amateur heat," Adrian confided. "Your favorite boy."

Diana took a huge bite of her burger, then offered it to him. "I hope you cream that asshole."

Adrian hesitated, then took a bite of her burger. "He's not so bad."

"Just another harmless prick?" she challenged.

Adrian chewed thoughtfully. "That *is* what I think of him."

"You two are friends?"

"I feel I should lie and say no."

"Don't lie," Diana said quietly.

"We grew up in the same neighborhood," Adrian told her.

That doesn't explain anything, Diana thought.

"We spar every so often. He's cuckoo, you know? Fucked up. But yeah, he's harmless," Adrian said defensively. "Not everyone's blessed with brains *and* talent."

"Yeah, impressive," Diana snorted.

Adrian peered out the window. Diana tried to turn the conversation to safer ground. "You didn't sit next to Hector like he asked."

"Didn't feel like it," Adrian countered.

"He thinks you're a good fighter."

"Hector got me started."

Diana was surprised by the news. "Yeah? How come you don't still work with him?"

"I'd be fifty before I got a pro fight with Hector,"

Adrian scoffed. "Cal manages me through the amateur stuff so I can make my move sooner." He picked at his salad. "No sense doing this unless I make some money, right? I can't work for my dad forever."

"True." Instinctively Diana understood what was driving him. In a way, she and Adrian were alike.

Adrian seemed to feel the same way. "My little brother—right outta school, he enlists in the marines." He looked at Diana. "No, thank you. Anyway, I don't think Hector ever believed in me. But he's probably different with you."

"Why?"

"You're a girl."

Wrong answer. Diana looked down and grabbed her breasts. "I am? Are you sure? This could be a problem."

Adrian nervously averted his eyes.

"I may have to cut these off, huh?" Diana goaded him. "I mean, to be a fighter?"

Completely unsettled, Adrian threw up his hands and looked out the window. "Stop foolin'—"

Eyes blazing, Diana let go of her breasts. "Who's fooling?"

Things got quiet after that. Adrian paid the check

and they walked to the subway, talking about music and movies they liked.

They took the D train back to Brooklyn.

Diana and Adrian sat in a nearly empty subway car, a seat between them. The roaring clatter softened as the train rose out of the tunnel onto the Manhattan Bridge. The skyline views on both sides of the river were spectacular, the brightly lit seaport against the looming Manhattan skyline on one side, and across the river, Brooklyn's dark warehouses and waterfront streets.

Diana stood and looked out the window. "Wanna see where my mom was born?" she asked quietly.

"Sure." Adrian stood at her side, close to her. Diana pointed to a group of buildings in Manhattan, near the water.

"Right there. Thirty-seven years ago."

They were silent for a moment. Adrian looked down at the black water of the East River, resting his hands on the glass windows. His knuckles were swollen and raw. Without thinking, Diana ran her hand over them. "Your hands are all fucked up."

He took his hands away from the glass and examined them. "Cal wraps them too tight when I spar."

Their heads were close as they looked at his hands. The black girders of the bridge flashed and flickered past the window until finally, their eyes met.

"You should tell him to go easy on you," Diana said softly. She liked the way his face looked in the passing lights.

"Maybe."

The train shot back underground, and the metallic roar made it difficult to talk. Diana liked the fact that they didn't have to say much.

Later, when they reached her apartment complex, they sat on the steps, their faces silhouetted against the green fluorescent light of the lobby.

"So what kinda name is Adrian?"

He looked away. "This is the story of my life."

"What?" Diana said innocently.

"Nothing. You want to know about my name."

"I just asked you."

"Okay," he said slowly. "My mom, when she was pregnant with me, she didn't . . . you know, she wasn't sure if it was a boy or a girl." He looked down at his feet. When he looked up again he was smiling. "But she's all like crazy superstitious, right? She has to name what's in her belly so it has a soul and shit.

94

So she gives me a name for either a boy or a girl. But it's *obviously* for a girl," he added ruefully.

"No it's not." Diana was sorry she'd brought it up. Still, she liked hearing about his mom.

"It'd be like your mom naming you Juan."

"Not really." Diana wondered why her mother had chosen her name. Her father never talked about stuff like that.

"But close."

Diana looked at him. "I like your name. I like saying it."

For a moment he didn't say anything. Then he slowly leaned over and lightly swatted at her leg. "This is different. Usually I only see you surrounded by sweaty guys."

"I sweat, too."

"So I've noticed."

That one stung but Diana shrugged it off. "Some joker."

A car entered the apartment complex, its lights crawling along the narrow road. They watched it go past, leaving them in shadow again.

"You didn't have to walk me home," Diana said, as the car's red taillights faded.

"I don't mind."

"I mean, I can take care of myself."

"I know," Adrian said, examining his knuckles. "I wanted to."

Why do you always have to be a hardass? Diana asked herself. She tried a safer topic. "So, what's it like in Gowanus?"

"My neighborhood? It's great," Adrian said sarcastically. "These kids in my building, fourteen or fifteen maybe, they're chasing each other outside, playing like cowboys and Indians. Like kids, right? Shooting guns at each other for fun." He shook his head at the thought. "And they weren't even enemies! Just playing around, the stupid shits."

He glanced at her to make sure she understood. "One's got a hole in his lung the size of a quarter. Other's got a leg he can't even walk on. Real guns. Loaded."

Diana wasn't surprised. "That's messed up. Guess stuff like that happens all the time."

Adrian looked up at the boxlike buildings cutting out the sky. "In these places—no one matters."

"No one and nothing," Diana agreed.

Adrian clenched his fist. "That's not gonna be my life, man," he said fervently. "I'm gonna turn pro and move far away from here. Someplace where I'm not gonna get killed doing my laundry."

"Yeah, right?" Diana chimed in. "Or get raped in your own fucking stairway—"

Adrian imitated a TV newscaster. "Shot dead for a pair of shoes—"

Diana sighed. "Pathetic."

"Happy times," Adrian said grimly.

They both started to laugh. Diana felt good talking to Adrian, as if she had known him for a long time. She glanced at him sideways.

"That girl who's been at the gym to watch you spar, all dolled up—she your girlfriend now?" she asked, trying to sound casual.

Adrian shrugged. "Karina? Sometimes."

Diana lifted her brows in mock surprise. "She's your sometimes girlfriend?"

"I mean, you know, it's cool between us."

Diana didn't know. And it was bothering her. "She's pretty."

"Yeah, she is. She's sweet on me but I don't have the time to be like, you know . . ."

". . . be a Romeo," Diana said, feeling better.

His face brightened. "Yeah. I step off when she gets all intense. Half the time I get a feeling she only likes me cuz I wanna go pro."

"You feeling exploited?" Diana teased.

"I'm serious!" Adrian said sharply. "She's gorgeous and all, but it's like, sometimes we don't have too much to say to each other, you know?"

"Sounds like a dream date for most guys."

Adrian smiled. "Yeah, right. I guess I don't know what I'm supposed to be looking for anymore—"

"Well, what do you *want?*" Diana asked intently.

He took a deep breath and squinted up at the dark sky. "Fuck if I know."

They sat there in silence for a few moments. Then Adrian suddenly leaned close to Diana and kissed her hesitantly. Their mouths seemed to explode when they touched.

Blood racing, she pulled back. "Why did you do that?"

"I don't know." Adrian put his hand on her neck and gently pulled her closer. He kissed her again, deeply. Diana felt her emotions surging. She felt light-headed, teetering between excitement and uncertainty.

"You taste sweet," Adrian whispered.

"Hmm, I think of myself as salty," Diana managed.

"Wrong. You're sweet."

Diana moved closer. "So are you." As they kissed

again, Adrian's hand moved over her breast and stayed there.

"Please don't cut these off."

Laughing, she moved his hand away. "You're too much." But she actually needed to recover. Her heart was pounding against her chest and she had trouble catching her breath.

They fell silent again. A moment later they kissed, as if drawn together by an invisible string. This time Diana was ready for the electric rush of sensation and emotion that flooded through her. But she wasn't ready for what happened next.

Adrian abruptly broke away.

"I gotta go," he said, his voice husky. He stood up and moved down the stairs. "I'll talk to you soon."

"Yeah," Diana said, but she was totally confused. Heart pounding like a thousand speedbags, she watched him run down the stairs and disappear onto the street. *What happened?* she wondered, slowly moving into the lobby.

Later, as she tossed restlessly in bed, Diana kept asking the same question.

Chapter 7

Diana loosened up, preparing to spar with a young fighter called Frisco. She shook out her arms and legs, cracked her neck, and bounced on her toes, more confident and centered in her body than ever before.

"He's gonna go after you," Hector warned. "That opens him up. Get him when he's open."

She nodded, eyes on her opponent. The bell rang and she advanced to the center of the ring. Frisco was aggressive, but Diana swiftly ducked and moved, avoiding most of his punches. After a minute, Frisco lost his cool and began throwing punches wildly. When he did make contact, Diana absorbed the blow.

A few boxers and trainers had gathered to watch.

Don leaned on his cane and nodded at Hector. "She's got a good chin."

"I know," Hector said proudly. *The kid's come a long way,* he thought, watching her handle Frisco.

There was a commotion near the entrance. Everyone except Hector and the two boxers in the ring turned to see what was happening.

"Hey, champ," someone yelled.

The current middleweight champion, Cody Grant, was making a surprise visit to his roots. It was as if someone had turned up the lights in the drab gym. People dashed over to greet him as he strode inside, flanked by bodyguards, diamonds glinting on his fingers and wrists. The champ looked surprisingly young in person, and extremely slick. His tailored clothes and expensive jewelry were in sharp contrast to the torn sweat clothes and shabby gear of the hopefuls crowding around for a glimpse of the champ—one of them who had fought his way out of Brooklyn, to the promised land.

Hector remained at the ropes, watching Diana. Both fighters stepped back, momentarily distracted by the champ's noisy entrance. Reflexively, Diana glanced aside.

"Pay attention!" Hector warned. Too late. Frisco caught Diana square in the face.

She countered with a wicked left hook that surprised him, then fired another combination before he could get set. Diana's face was swollen where Frisco hurt her, but she became more aggressive. *Can't teach that,* Hector thought. *Mark of a true fighter.*

Later, Hector checked Diana's eye in his office. He gently turned her face to the bright fluorescent light. "Let's see here," he murmured. He probed the swollen area and she flinched. "Frisco really popped you one."

"Popped him back, didn't I?"

Hector smiled. "You're getting the hang of this game." He began applying an oily salve to the purple area around her eye. "You should get your own gloves soon," he suggested. "And some decent shoes."

Diana groaned. "I'm poor enough as it is."

"Well, you gave this guy an honest fight today. You should have your own gloves."

Diana realized Hector was paying her a compliment. Before she could respond, Diana heard a knock and turned.

Adrian stood shyly at the half-open door. "Hey, Hector," he greeted the trainer. He paused awkwardly and looked at Diana. "You gonna walk home?"

Diana nodded, then turned to Hector. "I'm taking off."

"See you later," Hector said as she walked out with Adrian. But she didn't hear a word.

Hector went to his desk and took a clipboard from his drawer. On it was a newsprint listing of amateur fighters—and a booklet called "The New York Gender-Blind Amateur Boxing Initiative."

The kid deserves her chance in the ring, Hector thought, flipping through the booklet.

When they were well out of sight of the gym, Adrian moved close to Diana and quickly kissed her swollen cheek.

"Ow . . ." Diana pulled away.

"Sorry. Forgot."

They continued walking, both of them carrying their gym bags.

"My first battle scar," Diana said quietly. She was still glowing with pride at Hector's compliment.

Adrian smiled and leaned closer. "It's beautiful."

When they reached Diana's building they walked over to the outdoor playground in the back. It was dark except for a single flickering streetlight that was about to burn out. Adrian leaned against the metal bars of a jungle gym and put his arms around Diana's waist. The moment he touched her Diana's heart began racing.

Diana glanced up at her building. "My dad'll give me grief if I keep coming home so late."

"Does he know . . ."

Adrian's question churned up conflicting emotions. She felt elated, uncertain, curious and wary at the same time. She also felt a bit scared.

"About what?" Diana asked, needing to hear.

Adrian pulled her closer. "This?"

"Not unless he's holding binoculars this very second."

They stepped away from each other, spooked by the possibility. Diana gave him a small, nervous shove, needing to touch him again.

"So what is 'this'?" she asked quietly. In the brief silence that followed Diana could hear her booming heartbeat.

Adrian shrugged and glanced away. "Who knows."

Honest answer, Diana thought. She ran her hand down his neck. "You still like me with my black eye?"

Adrian smiled. "I think I like you more."

His kiss ignited her senses like a grass fire in a high wind. Her emotions were seething, tumbling from hunger to fear as his arms folded around her. Then there was nothing but the breathless silence and their bodies melting together in the shadows.

Standing in his darkened bedroom, Sandro stood at the window. He tried to keep his emotions contained as he watched Adrian and Diana kiss in the playground below. *It's normal,* he told himself. But Diana was his little girl. He had to protect her. *She doesn't have a mother to teach her,* Sandro brooded. *A boyfriend is one thing, stealing is serious.*

When Diana entered the apartment she went straight to the kitchen. She opened the refrigerator door and began picking through various leftovers.

Sandro stood in the doorway, watching her.

"Hi, Dad," Diana said casually. She started stacking plastic containers on the counter.

Sandro tried to keep his voice calm. "You stole money from me."

Diana's shoulders slumped and she nodded, voice husky with regret. "I'm gonna pay you back—"

"And who's the kid you're running around with?"

Diana sighed. Her father had been watching from the window. "Just someone."

"That who you sneak out with after school?" The question had a nasty edge.

Diana recognized her father's tone. It meant he was close to losing it. "Dad," she said softly.

When she turned, Sandro saw the purple bruise on her face. He stared at her fresh black eye, his chest heaving with rage. "What the hell happened to you?"

Diana didn't know what to say. She smiled and touched her face to show it wasn't really serious.

"Did *he* do this to you?"

"Adrian?" she blurted, suddenly alarmed. "No. Listen—"

But her father wasn't listening. Bristling with anger, he rushed at Diana.

"How could you let him do this?"

Instinctively she covered up and stepped back. "Get away from me, Dad."

"That's how it goes? You hook up with a creep who knocks you around?"

"Oh, what?" Diana dropped her hands in disbelief. "You're so reformed now, you give *me* advice?"

"I won't let this happen to my daughter."

"You let it happen to your wife."

It was like a right hook. Sandro froze, unable to speak. He heard a shuffling sound behind him.

Tiny stood in the doorway, watching them. "What's going on?"

"Go to your room," Diana said wearily.

"You're not my mother."

Sandro turned. "Get outta here, Tiny."

Tiny stood his ground. "No."

"You heard me!" Exasperated, Sandro lunged at him, but Diana swiftly stepped in front of her brother.

"Don't you fucking touch him."

Sandro shoved her aside, but Diana didn't budge. Her body coiled with raw anger.

Tiny ran back to his room and slammed the door shut.

Diana glared at her father. "Think if Mom was around she'd give me the same wise words? She lasted long enough being your target practice. Till the end I never would've thought she hated you the way she did."

Sandro didn't realize Diana hated him so much. He wasn't proud of himself, but he tried his best to keep it together, to protect his family. "Do you starve?" he asked hoarsely. "Do you have clothes on your back? I made some mistakes, but I am not a bad parent. I can take care of my kids."

"Yeah, and maybe we'll blow our brains out, too, 'cause of you."

"That's it. You're grounded."

Diana glared at her father with contempt. "Oh yeah, right—"

Enraged, Sandro shoved her hard against the wall. "Give me back what you took from me. And if I ever see you with that guy again, I swear to God I'll—"

"You'll what, Dad—you'll fucking *kill* me?"

With startling force Diana shoved him aside and stormed past him.

Breathing hard, Sandro stood alone in the kitchen as another door slammed. *How did it get like this?* he asked in silence. But there was no answer.

Seething with anger, Diana paced back and forth in the semidarkness of her room like a caged animal. She pounded her fists against the wall as if hitting the heavy bag. The motion of her body and the velocity of her hands found a rhythm of their own and she began to shadowbox, throwing beautifully agile combinations. She glimpsed her reflection in the mirror, face intent, hands darting like snakes.

Soon she was loose and sweating, but the workout didn't help. Diana could feel the tension through the walls of her room. She knew her father's pattern. Soon he'd go out, drink a few beers, and stew for an hour or so. Then he'd come back and start banging on her door.

Sure enough, a few minutes later Diana heard the front door click shut. Her father was off to the corner bar.

Impulsively, Diana decided to leave the house as well. But first, she needed to make a phone call. It took her a long time to work up the courage to dial Adrian's number.

Thoughts and feelings careening, Diana ran all the way, through darkened streets lit by trash fires and occasional taxi lights. She followed her regular jogging route to the Gowanus housing project where Adrian lived with his parents.

The aftermath of the confrontation with her father had left her deeply depressed. But the prospect of being with Adrian energized her drained emotions. As instructed, she went into building 14 and took the stairs to the third floor.

Diana knocked softly at apartment 9. The door

opened a crack and Adrian peered at her. She was sweating and breathless. "I ran," she whispered.

"I can see that." He put a finger to his lips and let her inside. Adrian was barefoot and wearing a robe. "My parents are light sleepers," he whispered.

They tiptoed down the hall to Adrian's bedroom. It was small but neat.

Adrian sat on the bed. Diana looked around. There were no chairs. She moved to the window, then came back and sat beside Adrian. Their nearness set her heartbeat racing.

"So, what happened?" he asked quietly.

Diana shook her head, unable to express the emotions boiling through her thoughts. She buried her face in his neck, inhaling his warm scent. After a moment she grabbed his collar. "I'm afraid I'll take advantage of you in this robe," she whispered.

"But I'm defenseless," Adrian protested.

She kissed his neck and ears. "I thought you were a fighter."

"My parents are in the next room."

Diana ran her hands across his chest and down his spine. "They probably do this, too."

Adrian winced. "I try not to think about that."

"Can I stay here tonight?" Diana asked huskily, heart booming.

He looked away as if trying to decide. Finally he nodded. "But no monkey business."

Mocking his serious tone, Diana moved away from him with an elaborate flourish. But underneath she was hurt. "I thought all guys jumped at this chance," she said ruefully. "So maybe I'm not prime trim."

Adrian's eyes went wide in amazement. He softly tackled Diana and rolled on top of her so their faces were inches apart. "How'd you get so fucking crude?" he asked gently. But she could see he was truly baffled.

Diana snorted. "How'd you get so fucking *polite?*"

"Shut up," Adrian said, kissing her. His hands began to search her body, and Diana felt her breath coming faster. She was swept up by a violent hunger that threatened to burst through all restraint. Suddenly he rolled off her.

Diana groaned. "You're serious."

"Cal told me to keep a lid on it till I fight Ray."

Diana paused, intrigued by the news. "So, you two are gonna go at it."

"It's just a preliminary—local stuff."

She moved closer. "And that 'no sex' stuff is for real?"

Adrian heaved a weary sigh. "It's for real—let's sleep."

"Yeah, yeah," she muttered. Diana took off her shoes and socks, Adrian took off his robe, and they both got under the covers. They lay there for a moment, warm and delicious. Diana struggled to smother her smoldering desire for Adrian.

"Are your parents still together?" Adrian asked.

Diana snuggled closer. "Not really. My mom died. Long time ago."

"Oh. What happened? If you don't mind—"

"She killed herself."

Diana could feel Adrian shrink back. "Man," he said softly. "I'm sorry."

"Me, too." The memory chilled her emotions.

After a moment she turned to look at him, their faces very close. "It's nice," she whispered.

Adrian didn't get it. "Hmnnn?"

"To look forward to you."

"You mean . . ."

"I mean all of it," Diana told him. She still felt a raging desire for more, but just being together was heaven.

He closed his eyes. "Dream of me knocking out Ray in three."

"I already have," she murmured.

A moment later they both drifted off to sleep, safe in each other's arms.

Diana returned home at dawn. She was relieved to find her father was still asleep. There was a half-empty wine bottle on the kitchen table.

She went to her room and began packing a suitcase. A few minutes later she heard a soft knock at the door. Tiny peeked inside.

"Can I come in?"

Diana continued packing. "Yeah."

Tiny sat on the bed, watching her. "Taking a vacation?"

"I'm off to the islands," Diana said ruefully. She didn't look at her brother. Actually, she didn't know where she was going. This thing with her father's money made it impossible. She'd stolen and he would make her pay for it forever. *I only took what he should have given me*, she thought bitterly. But she wouldn't let her father ruin her relationship with Adrian. Maybe she could stay with Marisol until she got a job.

Tiny threw a pillow at her. "Come on, this is melodrama."

"You don't even know what that word means."

"*Please*," Tiny corrected. He stood up and began to recite. "Melodrama—a story told with extravagant emotions."

Diana was impressed. "So you're the brain, so what?"

"I didn't mean it like that." He gave her a sly smile. "I hear it's true. You got a *luv-ah.*"

"Aw, man . . ." Diana groaned.

"First comes love—then comes marriage!" her brother teased.

Diana threw a punch, missing on purpose.

"Sensitive!" Tiny ducked away, laughing.

Diana sat on the bed next to him, staring ahead. "It's not funny."

Tiny's grin faded. He knew she was serious about this guy, whoever he was. This constant war with their father was tearing him and Diana apart, but he didn't want to lose his sister.

Tiny reached into his pocket and tossed a roll of bills into Diana's lap.

She looked at the money, then at him, confused.

"I don't know how you pay Hector. Don't think I

want to know." Tiny said, shaking his head. "Dad's wasting his money on me. He'll never have to know if you use it instead."

Diana put her arm around her brother, her desperation and fear washed away by a flood of gratitude. She took a deep breath. She could pay back her father.

"What'll you do when you're supposed to be at the gym?" Diana asked softly.

Tiny yawned and stood up. "I'm a geek—I'll do something constructive with my time." He moved to the door and paused. "Popi doesn't know you were out all night," Tiny said, as he left the room.

Diana pushed her suitcase to the floor and crawled under the covers, but she couldn't sleep. All she could think about was being close to Adrian.

Chapter 8

Hector lived in a small brick house in Queens.

Diana felt nervous as she approached the front stairs. This was her first adult party. She could hear music and laughter inside. Looking through the window she saw Hector at a table, wearing a cone-shaped birthday hat, mixing drinks for his guests. He looked ridiculous. Diana rang the bell.

A plump, pretty brunette woman opened the door. She gave Diana a warm smile. "You're the new boxer. I'm Candice."

"Hi," Diana said shyly. She followed Candice inside. The house was cluttered with plants in every windowsill and flowers on the table. Hector stood at the table with his pals Al and Tino. Diana spotted Ray talking to Don. The trainer raised his beer to her.

As Diana looked around the room, other trainers and fighters nodded in recognition. She was both surprised and flattered. Even Al and Tino, who were totally indifferent to her at the gym, seemed happy to see her when she approached the table.

"Happy birthday," she greeted Hector.

Hector gave her a big grin. "I was just talking about you."

"I've come to defend myself." She crouched in a boxer's stance.

"Tonight, I only have kind words for you."

"Oh—you must be drunk."

Al and Tino chuckled, but Hector became serious. "I am a little. But I'm happy tonight." He put his arm around Candice. "I have a wife who puts up with me. I got a house, good friends. I have my work . . ."

"Not bad for an old man," Diana agreed.

Hector looked at his pals. "Always insulting the elders." Then he gave Diana a curious smile. "Remember I said girls can't be boxers?"

"I remember."

"Girls—excuse me, *women*—have a lower center of gravity. Maybe they're more grounded once they build strength. Makes 'em a different kind of boxer."

"You serious?" Tino said, glancing at Al.

Hector lifted his hand. "Just a theory. Way to prove it is to get more girls in the ring. Like any other fighter." He pointed a finger at Diana. "You could be as good as some of those guys at your weight. You should compete."

"Don't worry," Candice advised. "I've seen him like this. It'll pass."

But later Hector was still enthusiastic about his plan for Diana. He confided that he was going to try to arrange a match for her. "But it's got to be the right division. What's your weight?" he asked her.

"I dunno. One twenty-one, maybe."

Hector took Diana into the bathroom and put her on the scale. "One twenty-six." He congratulated her. "All that muscle you're building."

"What's the division?"

"You're a featherweight. Perfect. We'll register you for the next amateur heat. It's good practice."

Diana stepped off the scale and flexed her biceps in a muscle pose. "I'm a featherweight." She felt like Cinderella. Things had gotten a lot better since the day Hector had refused to train her. And she definitely felt a lot better about herself. All her problems were still there, but she felt she could learn to solve them—one by one.

Not only was Hector a good trainer, he was a great host. The food was good, the beer was cold, and the music was hot. Diana sat in a corner observing the festivities. She was enjoying herself, but she really didn't have much to say. She wondered if Adrian was coming.

Hector moved across the floor and executed a slick salsa cross step in front of her.

"Fancy moves."

Hector smiled and bowed. "Hey—you're learning from the best."

The front door opened. Diana's stomach tightened when she saw Adrian. He walked into the living room, greeting Candice and the other boxers, working his way over to where Hector stood.

When their eyes met, Diana smiled. Adrian smiled back, but he seemed remote.

"You made it," Hector said warmly.

"Happy birthday." Adrian handed him a small, wrapped box.

"What's this?" Hector asked as he opened it.

"A trinket."

Inside was a pair of tiny silver boxing gloves hanging from a chain. Hector beamed, delighted with the gift.

"For your rearview mirror," Adrian explained.

"It's a good luck charm?"

"Let's say if I'm the next featherweight champ, it gives good luck to all who cross its path. If not, we're doomed."

"You a poet or a boxer?" Diana asked.

"I'm a poet *when* I box," Adrian said, nose in the air.

"Oh, excuse me."

Hector gave Adrian a bear hug. "Thank you."

"It's nothing."

A Spanish love song began to play. Adrian and Diana glanced at each other. Diana kept wishing he would come over to talk to her, but Adrian moved to the other side of the table and began sampling the food.

Diana walked into the kitchen. As she stood sipping a beer, she could hear the party moving into full swing. She was confused by Adrian's coolness. *Guess he doesn't want anybody to know,* Diana thought. She would talk to him later.

The door swung open, and Diana glimpsed Hector dancing with Candice. Ray entered and squished past her to get to the refrigerator. He pulled out a beer and stared at her. Diana turned away.

"You're not mingling," Ray observed.

"What?"

"It's a party. You should be dancing."

"I'm not much of a dancer."

"Sure you are." Weaving drunkenly, Ray started boxing around her. "You know how to dance."

"Hector says my footwork gets sloppy."

"Looks okay to me. Come on. Let's box."

Diana edged away. "Not in Hector's kitchen."

Ray smirked. "But you're all serious and shit." He threw a punch. "Come on—be a man."

Suddenly Diana couldn't stand to be in the same room with him. As she moved to the door, Ray grabbed her arm.

"They say love kills you in the ring," he said hoarsely.

Diana yanked free and went into the living room, looking for Adrian. Then she saw him.

It was like someone punched her in the belly, driving the breath from her body. Adrian was in a corner talking to Karina—his "sometimes girl-friend." Diana's face was a mask as she watched them, but the blood was pounding through her stomach. Through the crowd Diana saw Karina's delicate hands and painted fingernails touch Adrian's arm. Karina brushed her long hair off her bare shoulders and lowered her bright eyes to meet Adrian's. Then a couple moved between them, and all Diana could see was Karina's gold ankle bracelet above black high heels. The couple parted, revealing Karina whispering in Adrian's ear.

Adrian looked up and saw her. Diana returned an icy stare. For a moment he seemed paralyzed. Then he turned and started kissing Karina.

Emotions crumbling, Diana moved blindly to the front door. Her expression was blank, but her insides were twisted with pain. Hector stood at the door talking to some guests, his hands waving, his smile animated.

"I gotta go, Hector," Diana said, squeezing past him.

Hector reached out to stop her. "But you just got here. Sure you can't stay longer?"

If I stay any longer I'll explode, Diana thought. She shook her head. "No, no . . . I'll see you at the gym."

"Well, all right, but I mean it—let's get you into fighting shape."

"Yeah," Diana said, edging to the door. "Sounds good."

Diana ran outside before anyone could see her face. She hadn't cried for a long time. Not since her mother died.

Diana couldn't remember exactly how she made it home. Still numb with pain, she quietly entered the apartment. Her father was on the couch, asleep in front of the TV. As she moved to her room she brushed a chair. Her father blinked awake.

"I gave up on you hours ago," he said sternly.

She paused and reluctantly came back to the living room.

"You know you're still grounded," Sandro reminded her.

Silently, Diana sat beside him on the couch.

"You saw that kid again."

"Yeah," Diana said wearily. "Am I grounded for life now?"

"Listen to me—"

Diana groaned softly. "Could you just lay off me for one night? There's nothing between me and him."

Sandro started to speak, but something in his daughter's voice held him back. He slumped on the couch and stared at the TV. "You're too young for this stuff anyway," he said finally.

"How old were *you*?"

Sandro half-smiled. "I was too young."

Diana didn't get it. Her brain was numb with hurt. "Huh," she murmured. "So it's my turn to make mistakes."

Hector brought his leftover birthday cake to the gym.

Don and Al stood nearby munching the cake as Hector fastened Diana's headgear. She threw a few punches, trying to loosen up.

"It was better with the ice cream," Don remarked, his mouth full.

"Christ." Hector shook his head and looked at Diana. "How do you feel?"

"Tired." It was true. Diana hadn't slept much after the party. But she was glad she'd decided to come to the gym. Hector had set her up with a special sparring partner—Adrian.

"Just stay steady," Hector instructed her. "Move your head and work your combinations when you find an opening."

Diana nodded, anticipating Adrian's arrival in the

ring. She slammed her gloves together, trying to control her surging emotions.

Cal approached the ring, his face tight with disapproval. "This is a waste of time," he told Hector. "Adrian's got a match coming up. I don't mean to insult you"—he glanced at Diana—"but—"

"What's the big deal?" Hector snorted, looking surprised. "There's nobody near Adrian's weight to spar with today. May as well give my girl a chance."

"I don't like it, Hector."

"Tell Adrian to think of her as a warm-up," Hector offered.

He already does, Diana thought, anxious to see Adrian step inside the ring.

Cal reluctantly climbed through the ropes and waved Adrian over.

Diana kept her eyes down, jogging in place, while Cal fastened Adrian's headgear. She looked up and saw Adrian give her a cautious glance. Both of them looked away.

"This equality crap has gone too far," Cal ranted.

"Should we just forget it?" Adrian said hopefully.

"No." Cal lowered his voice. "Get rough on her the first round and Hector'll stop it early."

Adrian's heart sank. There was no way he could follow Cal's instructions.

The start bell rang. Adrian and Diana moved to the center of the ring. Diana stared at him, eyes as blank as ice. They touched gloves and began to move around each other.

Diana tried a few jabs that Adrian avoided easily. But he stayed defensive, unwilling to throw a punch. For some reason that stirred all of Diana's pent-up rage. She came at him more aggressively, smacking his jaw with a hook, then his gut with an uppercut. Adrian leaned on the ropes, absorbing the blows.

"Come on!" Cal yelled. "What'd I tell you?"

"Hit me," Diana grunted, jabbing at him. He just stood there, covering up, ducking. Diana hit him with every combination she knew. He just took it.

"I said, hit me!" Diana yelled, trying to goad him. She stopped and turned to Hector. "I'm not gonna do this if he won't fight."

Hector looked at Adrian, then at Cal. "Well?"

Diana glared at Adrian, her face as cold as granite. "Wanna call it quits?" she sneered.

"Both of you, enough bullshit!" Hector warned. "Now box!"

Adrian sighed and advanced to the center of the

ring. Diana moved swiftly, energized by her anger. Adrian seemed more focused, avoiding her combinations. Finally he threw a quick jab that hit her in the face.

Adrian paused. "You all right?"

Diana stepped back, then came at him, eyes locked on his. His jab popped her again.

"Stay inside!" Hector shouted. "Don't just stand there!"

The sparring became serious. Diana started to bob and weave, feinting, then throwing fast combinations. Adrian countered with a powerful jab and hook, which Diana slipped, surprising him with a left uppercut. Adrian tagged her with a double hook to the body, driving her back. They exchanged a flurry of quick blows, then exhausted, draped their arms around each other in a sweaty headlock.

Diana leaned close to his face. "I love you," she whispered hoarsely.

Adrian's body stiffened, and he pushed her off. When he tried to punch she slipped inside and clinched. For a long moment their bodies clung together in a desperate, angry embrace. "I really love you," she said breathlessly.

Abruptly Diana broke away and slammed his face

with a hard left hook. Before he could counter, the bell rang, ending the round.

Adrian stole a glance at Diana as Cal squirted water into his mouth.

Hector took out Diana's mouthpiece and gave her water. "Okay, you're a good match for each other. You're strong on the offensive, but he's fast. Keep the defensive moves small. He goes after you, slip, feint, then BAM! Fool him."

"Whaddaya say, Hector," Cal called across the ring. "Enough foolishness for one day?"

"She's doing fine," Hector said loudly.

Diana stood in her corner, energized and ready to fight. "Let's go!"

Cal rolled his eyes in exasperation.

The start bell rang, and Diana shuffled forward. But within thirty seconds her exhaustion returned, and her anger was drained. She and Adrian spent the rest of the round jabbing and weaving.

When the round was over, they left the ring without looking at each other.

Later, after changing into fresh clothes, Diana came into Hector's office.

The trainer didn't notice her. He sat at his desk,

absorbed in a booklet titled "The Amateur Boxing Initiative."

Diana cleared her throat. "You were right about the defensive stuff," she declared. "He coulda had me there a couple times."

Hector beamed at her proudly. "You're still standing." He waved the booklet. "The important thing is to get you into this prelim coming up."

"Who's in my division?"

"Girls from other gyms. *Lots* of guys. Here . . . look at this." He tossed the booklet in her direction.

Diana caught it and skimmed through the pages. A few headlines caught her attention: "Experimental Bouts," "Gender-Blind Programs." What it meant was that she could compete, just like in any other sport.

Exhilarated by the prospect of real competition, Diana left the gym and started walking briskly down the street. She felt calmer, the pain and anger of Adrian's betrayal under control.

"Diana!" The sound of Adrian's voice shattered her control. Emotions churning, she glanced back and saw him coming out of the gym, still in his workout clothes. Unable to decide what to do, Diana kept walking.

"Diana," he called again. When she didn't turn around he shouted, "I'm not gonna run after you if that's what you want!"

Oh—I'm supposed to stop when you call, Diana fumed as she hurried to the bus stop. *Is that love or dog training?*

Chapter 9

It was Physical Fitness Day at Diana's high school. The entire gym class was herded out to the track behind the school. When the coach announced the first event the girls squinted at her as if she were insane.

"A mile's not gonna kill any of you," the coach growled. "Come on. That time of the year, ladies. Time for the President's . . ."

"I don't give a shit what the President thinks about my physical fitness," Veronica grumbled, joining Marisol at the start line. They waited sullenly, both muttering complaints. Diana wasn't bothered by the event; she ran four miles every morning.

The whistle blew. Groaning, the girls began shuffling forward. Diana moved to the head of the pack, running the mile at a nice easy pace that left her refreshed. She wasn't even breathing hard when she crossed the finish line first.

The push-up test was next. Most of the girls could barely do one. The coach shook her head sadly until she came to Diana. She was in the zone, doing one push-up after another, exerting steadiness and control.

At the pull-up bar the girls gathered to watch Diana as she completed ten reps with no visible effort.

"Those hormone treatments do the job," Veronica remarked, loud enough for Diana to hear.

A few months earlier Veronica's comment would have touched off a fight. But boxing had brought all of that under control. Diana realized she had achieved a new level, physically and mentally. She dropped from the bar and smiled at Veronica.

"Guzman—good work," the coach called. "You're top gun in class."

Diana paused to give Veronica a last, triumphant look before she walked away.

The school fitness test had left Diana feeling warm and loose, and she was early for her regular training workout with Hector. As usual lately, the trainer had his nose buried in a new fight schedule for sanctioned amateur bouts.

"Speedbag, heavy bag," he muttered, not looking up.

Hector followed her to the speedbags, looking up every so often to check her technique. But he could hear her at work. Diana rolled her fists smoothly and swiftly on the speedbag, keeping it hopping like a Ping-Pong ball. When they moved to the heavy bag, Diana kept banging left hook, right hand combinations that whacked the leather hard and fast. Hector nodded approval.

"Now that they're mixing up boys and girls you got a lot more opponents," he declared, with a trace of excitement. "They got you fighting a girl from Buffalo next week. And you can have a match every week if you want. None of this 'every four months' crap. It's like sex, you know?"

Laughing, Diana stepped away from the bag. "Hector—for real. How's it like sex?"

"You can think about it all you want, and even practice on your own. But you don't really know it till you getting busy with a partner."

"Whatever." Still laughing, Diana went back to

the heavy bag. But she kept thinking about what he'd said. Kept thinking about Adrian. *It's over,* she told herself, *get real.* Then she stopped thinking, and focused all her energy and will on the heavy bag. No matter who she fought—or loved—she'd be on her own, as always.

On the eve of her first real fight, Diana's nervousness was laced with anticipation. It would be her first real test against a fighter of her own weight, class, and gender.

Diana even had her first entourage. Tiny and Marisol had come with her to the Brooklyn Athletic Club, where the matches were being held. Diana was impressed with how much better the gym looked when they went upstairs. One of the trainers was at the door, taking admissions, and waved them by. The gym had been transformed for the event.

The floors were clean, and the front ring was surrounded by folding chairs. A large, disorganized crowd filled the gym. The refreshment stand was open, and kids with bad haircuts roamed around yelling, "Get your hot dogs here." A few older males hawked cold beer.

Tiny and Marisol moved to the still-empty seats

around the ring while Diana went back to her tiny closet to change. Along the way Diana saw trainers and boxers milling about, referees talking with judges, paunchy men throwing awkward punches at the heavy bag. *Looks like serious fans,* she thought, suddenly nervous.

Diana spotted a cop and a priest hunched together in somber conference. They both had their eyes on Ray, who was wearing his competition colors and smacking his gloves in frustration.

She slowed down to hear what they were saying. "Trainer says he's got a high fever," Don declared flatly. "He's dead on his feet with strep throat."

Ray stamped his foot like a child. "I'll fight that yellow jerk with one arm."

"Calm down," Don scolded. "There'll be other matches."

"Not soon enough." Ray stalked off, brushing past Diana.

She made her way to the back room, grateful for the quiet inside her closet. She had new shorts, and Hector had gotten her a deal on ring shoes. Nothing fancy but fresh. And the shoes felt good.

She walked into Hector's office to show him, but the trainer was deeply engrossed in his phone conversation. Diana shuffled around, wishing he'd finish. She looked at the photographs on the wall.

Hector's voice got loud and tight. "Let me get this straight; she's had three amateur matches and she's already going pro? Little premature, dontcha think?"

Diana studied an old photo of Adrian and Hector, arms around each other, smiling for the camera.

"Sure, there's a shortage of female talent, but that doesn't mean you put 'em in pro fights before they even got a feel for the ring." Hector waved his hands in exasperation. "What's the point of all this if they don't get amateur experience?"

Diana stared at a photo of Hector standing proudly behind a line of eager young boxers. One of the boys was Adrian.

"My girl fits the bill; she's young and she's got *defense* in her!"

Diana realized he was talking about her.

"Yeah. Tough break. Appreciate the call."

Hector hung up and shook his head. "Missy from Buffalo's thirty-three years old and can make some money as a pro. Why bother with small-fry stuff when you can be on TV?"

"It's totally called off?" Diana groaned. Now she

knew how Ray felt. *All dressed up and no place to fight,* she brooded.

Hector drummed his fingers on his desk, looking at her. Abruptly he stood up and hurried to the door. "Wait here a second!"

Diana followed and saw him rushing to talk to Ira.

"I gotta give people their ten bucks' worth, and half my fighters haven't even shown up," Ira ranted. He spotted Diana watching them and pointed. "Hey, what about her over there—her opponent's MIA, too."

Ira gestured at another female boxer standing nearby. The woman weighed at least a hundred and eighty pounds. Clearly she was much too big for Diana.

"She could be a light heavyweight, Ira," Hector scolded. "Come on, let's just see this thing in action."

"All right," Ira grumbled. "But if this thing gets ugly, you can't say I didn't warn you."

The triumphant expression on Hector's face suggested he had arranged a substitute.

"So . . . do I fight?" Diana asked expectantly.

He nodded. "You up to fight a guy?"

"Who?"

"Ray."

"Yeah," she said slowly, looking around at the noisy crowd. She watched Ira talking to Don and Ray. Ray glanced at her, and she knew the fight was on.

"This is for real," Hector warned.

"I hope so," Diana murmured, recalling that night in Hector's kitchen.

Diana stood at the rear of the gym, jogging in place while Hector rubbed her shoulders. She cracked her neck, then did a quick combination, shadowboxing.

"Loose?" Hector asked.

"Getting there," Diana lied. She felt as tight as shrink-wrap on a CD.

"Remember, you're judged on points," Hector instructed her. "Be aggressive about making legal punches." He began wrapping tape around her chest, over her tank top. "How's the tape feel?"

"A little tight."

"Breathe deep," Hector told her. "Stretch it out. Nervous?"

"No," she lied again.

Ira awkwardly climbed into the boxing ring. He was wearing a green satin tuxedo jacket that was too short, over rumpled brown pants. When he touched the microphone it set off a distorted whine.

"Welcome to Brooklyn A.C.," he recited from his index card. "In cooperation with the New York Amateur Boxing Initiative, let's welcome a new boxer to the ring. From Brooklyn, eighteen years old . . . one hundred twenty-five pounds . . . Diana Guzman."

Prodded by Hector, Diana started walking down the aisle. The audience gave her a smattering of applause. Tiny and Marisol were in the front row, clapping loudly as she climbed into the ring.

"Challenging Diana in the far corner, let's welcome Ray Cortez from Brooklyn. Nineteen years old . . . also one hundred twenty-five pounds."

Tiny and Marisol exchanged a horrified glance as Ray stepped into the ring wearing purple satin shorts. He started dancing around, arms raised in triumph, as if he had already won.

Ray's friends cheered loudly. But many other spectators were surprised, and a confused buzz circled the crowd.

"Both of these boxers' originally scheduled opponents couldn't make it," Ira explained, over the whining mike. "And these kids want to rumble! Let's give 'em a big hand for their fighting spirit!"

Ray banged his gloves together, grinning oddly at Diana across the ring. Hector caught the grin and didn't like it. He looked over at Ray's trainer. Don was looking at Ray with a worried expression. He'd caught the grin, too.

Ray and Diana advanced to the center of the ring, where the referee was waiting. The referee looked younger than Diana. He put his hands on their shoulders like in a football huddle. "You know the rules," he droned. "Let's keep it above the belt. Fight a fair fight and good luck."

Diana and Ray touched gloves and went back to their corners. The start bell rang, and Diana shuffled forward, gloves raised. "This is for real," Hector warned. "Cover up."

Ray came out aggressively, throwing punches at her face. Diana ducked and bobbed, avoiding most of the blows—but not all. Ray connected with a short right to her jaw, sending her back against the ropes. Ray lunged at her with a vicious hook, but Diana swiveled cleanly out of range. As he missed, Diana made solid contact with an uppercut to Ray's ribs. A few fans in the crowd clapped and cheered.

They circled each other. Ray's game plan seemed made of wild swings and intimidation. Diana tried to stay centered as he stalked her, taking small defensive steps. But something about his bristling energy got under her skin. Then they made eye contact, and Diana knew—Ray was out for blood.

Hector watched with grave attention. He also saw that Ray was out to prove something. He hoped he hadn't made a terrible mistake in setting up this match.

Diana threw a left hook, then drove a right into Ray's chin. Tiny jumped up and cheered. Ray swung wildly and finally landed a powerful jab, followed by a right to Diana's gut. The bell rang.

Diana fell into her chair, numb with exhaustion. Hector gave her water, and she spit into a bucket.

"Least he's predictable," Hector said ruefully.

"Yeah, he really wants to kill me."

"Okay, he's lunging, thinking you're gonna back away from him. Use that to throw your body shots."

"I'll try."

"Box, box!" Hector exhorted. "He wants to be scary, but you got better balance. Don't let go of him, and work your uppercuts."

Diana stood, ready to fight—then froze. Her father was standing in the back, his face grim as their eyes met. The bell rang and she shuffled forward, totally distracted. Ray immediately went for her face, and she couldn't move fast enough, taking some powerful blows.

The referee couldn't interfere. Ray moved in and she covered up, without throwing any punches. Ray jammed a left hook against her face, and she fell to the ground, stunned.

The referee stood over Diana and started to count.

"Stop the fight!" someone yelled.

To Diana the referee was a blurred figure. But his fingers were in focus, snapping off the count.

"Stop it—that's enough," people were shouting.

"Get up!" Marisol cried.

Diana used the ropes to get back on her feet, then rushed at Ray with a desperate combination. He stumbled back, grinning.

"You don't have it in you," Ray taunted.

"Hey, hey," the ref warned. "No talking!"

Diana's quick jab popped Ray in the nose, and suddenly they were going at it fiercely. Diana's hair was matted flat against her head, and bright red blood poured from her nose.

Sandro watched in disbelief. In the front row Marisol buried her head in Tiny's shoulder. "I don't have the stomach for this," she complained.

The bell rang, ending the round. The crowd

cheered the two boxers as they returned to their corners.

Marisol jumped to her feet. "Come on! Beat him to a pulp!"

Hector got eye to eye with Diana, dabbing her bloody nose with a cool, wet cloth. "Don't let him bully you like this! He wants to rattle your cage, and you just let him! Show him what you're made of!"

Diana nodded, practically weeping with exhaustion and pain. "He's a coward. I know that . . ." She looked up and saw her father walking out of the gym.

"You got better skills," Hector urged. "Use 'em now!"

The bell rang. Ray danced into the center. Diana advanced warily.

"Come on," Ray grunted. "I'm enjoying myself."

"No talking!" the ref warned.

Diana threw a jab, and Ray swung at her crotch. Ray's pals howled in delight.

The ref pulled Ray aside. "That's below the belt. This is a warning."

"What a prick!" Tiny yelled, jumping to his feet.

Marisol turned to him. "He can't do that, right?"

Ray and Diana resumed fighting. Diana landed some respectable jabs, but Ray suddenly tagged her with a right. She stumbled back and slipped a hook. Ray went for her gut, but she blocked him. Blatantly, he went for her groin again.

"Stop him!" Hector shouted, half in the ring.

The referee stepped between the boxers, holding Ray off. "Last warning . . . one more time, Cortez, and you're disqualified."

"Hey, what's below her belt anyway?" one of Ray's friends croaked loudly. "Nothin' but a *pussy!*"

"Shit," Ray said. "Wish I'd thought of that."

Diana lunged at Ray, but the ref held her back. "Hey! I gotta warn you, too?"

"Awww, for chrissakes . . . !" Hector called.

Pumped up with raw fury, Ray shoved Diana hard on the shoulder. The referee pulled her back. "That's it, Cortez!" the ref declared. "It's over!"

The referee lifted both hands in the air, indicating he was stopping the fight. A hush fell over the crowd. Don got into the ring and yanked Ray to his corner.

"I've had it with you, kid," Don said, voice heavy with disgust.

Slightly confused, Diana watched as the referee leaned over the ropes and conferred with the three judges who were scoring the match.

The crowd remained quiet as the referee whispered something to Ira. Clumsily, Ira climbed into the ring and took the microphone. "Ladies and gentlemen, in a unanimous decision, Ray Cortez has been disqualified."

A chorus of boos disputed the decision.

"And Diana Guzman is declared the winner in this preliminary featherweight match."

Tiny and Marisol began hopping up and down, cheering Diana's victory.

"We got some cruiserweights coming up," Ira went on, "and in the meantime, folks, support your local gym and buy more of those hot dogs!"

Ray's supporters continued to boo as Hector put his arms around Diana and escorted her out of the ring. Hector tried to appear enthusiastic even though he knew that for a boxer, this was not a pure victory. Flinching from the boos, Diana climbed through the ropes and walked out of the gym.

Hector followed Diana as she hurried down the stairs and stumbled outside. When Hector left the building, he saw Diana huddled on the curb, her nose a swollen mess, her body slumped in defeat.

Hector sat beside her. "He doesn't deserve to box," he said softly.

Diana turned her face away. "Ray fought better'n me till those fouls."

"But he disqualified himself," Hector persisted. "Ray knew all the rules and couldn't play by them."

"He wanted to destroy me," Diana muttered.

"He's too stupid to destroy you!" Hector countered triumphantly. "Come on! He had you on the ground, you got right up. He split your eye, you came back for more. Someone calls you a name— you attack!"

Hector put his arms around her. Diana leaned against him and closed her eyes.

"You know the trouble with you?" Hector said after a while.

Diana rolled her eyes, angrily pulling away. "O wise one, what's wrong with me now?"

Insulted by her attitude, Hector pointed a finger at her. "I'll tell you what's wrong. You can't keep your fight in the ring, and that's the only place it matters. That's the trouble with you. You don't have mental control of the game. If Ray hadn't fouled out first, *you* would have been for trying to hit him while the ref was breaking you up. Did you think about that?" Hector asked sharply.

He looked away and sighed. "The ref gets between you, you take a step back, take a breath and let go of the bullshit, 'cause you're above it, right?"

Diana stared silently at the ground.

"You already got power that no one expects," Hector pleaded. "It's your mind you gotta train the hardest."

Diana nodded, trying to absorb what he was telling her. Then she looked up, eyes blazing. "I coulda killed him right there! God! I shoulda backed off, but I just . . ."

"Diana," Hector said, his voice low and serious. "You're something else. You showed me you got heart. You do. You really got the stuff."

They sat silently for a long time, Hector's words circling Diana's thoughts like Christmas lights.

Diana wearily let herself into the apartment and headed for the kitchen.

Her father sat at the table, drinking wine. Their eyes met as she entered, then she turned and opened the refrigerator.

"All the time you've been sneaking around, and for what?" Sandro rumbled. "To get the shit beaten out of you, that's what."

Diana stared into the fridge. Her face was impassive, but she was about to explode. "Thanks a lot, Dad," she muttered.

Her father snorted derisively. "It makes me laugh. But you know, it was almost like *entertainment*—"

"Hey." Diana glared at him. "I won tonight."

Her father responded with a bored glance. He stood, holding the table for balance, then stumbled toward her.

Diana stood her ground, emotions churning. "I won," she repeated slowly. "Whaddaya think of that?"

"I think you're ridiculous."

"Why?"

" 'Cause you're no good!' he ranted, reeking of wine and tobacco. "You're nothing but a rotten street fighter. You looked like a loser in there—"

"Everything I know about losing I learned from you, Dad," Diana shot back.

Her quiet words were like a razor. Sandro blinked as if wounded. "Hey! I'm your father—"

"Some father! The only thing you had the heart to love you practically beat into the grave."

"Shut up with that," Sandro warned.

But Diana was beyond reason. Her boiling emotions were flooding over her control. "You just had to push her, didn't you?"

"I mean it—" Sandro growled, clenching his fist.

"Till she'd rather die than answer to you," Diana went on, goading him.

"I said shut up with that!"

Sandro swung at her wildly, but Diana was ready. She smacked his face with a short right that staggered him. Knees wobbly, he stumbled back.

Anger like a tornado roared through her brain, and Diana shoved her father hard. Stunned, he tried to retreat, but she shoved him again.

Sandro turned his head away, trying to hide the fear in his eyes. Diana started punching her father, years of repressed fury driving every blow. Sandro lumbered forward, too slow and drunk to fight back.

"This is a kick," Diana taunted. "For a loser like me."

"Stop it," her father groaned, slowly collapsing to the floor.

Swept up by deep rage, Diana kicked him in the gut. Sandro screamed and shielded himself. "Stop!"

But Diana couldn't hear anything except the anger howling through her head as she kicked him again. "Think I belong to you?" She grunted breathlessly. "I'm your property?"

The fury lifted her, and she fell on her father,

straddling him on the floor. She grabbed his head, lifting it with both hands. "I could snap your neck in half right now."

Sandro trembled in her grip, eyes fluttering as if about to faint.

Diana rattled his skull. "I could kill you if I felt like it."

"Please—"

"Mom begged. Did you stop when she said 'please'? I can't remember."

She dug her nails into his neck, drawing blood. The booming fury reached a triumphant crescendo. "You belong to me now," Diana said, gasping for breath. "How's it feel to see so much of yourself so close? Pretty sickening, huh?"

"Stop it, Diana. Please, stop!"

Tiny's voice punctured the yowling storm. Slowly, like air escaping a balloon, the anger drained.

Diana blinked, as if awakening, and saw Tiny at the doorway. Her brother's face was frozen with terror. Diana recognized the look from childhood, from those horrible nights when Sandro beat their mother. She slid her hands away from Sandro's neck and stood up.

Sandro rolled over, groaning. Tiny knelt beside him.

Shaking, Diana leaned against the wall, watching them. "All these years you just looked right through me," she rasped, breath ragged.

Her voice trailed off, and a thick blanket of silence settled over the kitchen.

Chapter 10

When Diana rang Hector's bell, Candice answered the door.

"Well, hi, come on in," Candice said, somewhat surprised. "Hector's inside."

Hector sat in the kitchen, reading the newspaper. He smiled quizzically when he saw Diana. "Well, look what the cat dragged in."

Diana stood in the doorway. "I need a place to stay," she said quietly.

Hector glanced at his wife. "Trouble at home?"

"Yeah."

Hector sighed. He knew Sandro's temper from the old days. "You can stay in the office," he said finally.

"I'll put a mattress down for you," Candice said. "Come with me."

Diana followed her to the small office, near the living room. She stood looking at the photographs on the wall, while Candice went to get the bedding. There was a shot of Hector as a young man, wearing swim trunks on the beach. Another of Hector and Candice in pastel wedding clothes. And one of Hector sitting at a table with three teenaged boys, their glasses raised in a toast.

"Who are they?" Diana asked, when Candice returned. "These boys, I mean."

Candice carefully set a single mattress on the floor. "Those are Hector's kids."

"Where are they?" Diana asked, dumbfounded.

Candice gave her a small, tight smile. "He doesn't see them too often."

That night, as Diana tried to sleep, she stared at the photo of Hector and his sons. *Doesn't anybody stay together anymore?* she wondered.

Adrian wished Karina could talk about something else beside herself.

It was all about her dress, her shoes, her nails, her needs. Adrian brooded as they sat together on a bench outside his apartment building. It was a sunny day and lots of people were strolling about. Salsa music blared from a nearby boombox.

Karina put her arm around him. "Hope you're thinking about me."

Adrian shrugged. "Oh yeah."

A group of teenagers drifted past their bench. The last one had corn-row hair, just like Diana. Startled, Adrian hopped off the bench. "Hey."

The teenager turned. It was a guy, a total stranger. Adrian lifted his hands. "Never mind."

When Adrian came back, Karina started playing with his hair. "Who was that?"

"Oh, nobody."

"You sure?" Karina persisted.

Adrian pulled away. "Quit it." He smiled, embarrassed. "Uh, look, Karina, I think maybe we need to talk."

"About what?" she asked suspiciously.

For once, not about you, Adrian thought.

After school Diana and Marisol walked outside to the front steps, where they sat talking. Marisol was still excited about Diana's win over Ray—and the fact that Diana had finished first in the fitness tests.

"You're so buff I can't stand next to you," Marisol teased. "Gonna sport some hype varsity threads soon?"

"Oh, please . . ." Diana yawned.

"I'm serious. This athletic shit makes you, like, a class achiever."

Diana gave Marisol a twisted grin. "Huh, now that I got school all covered, I only got the little world outside these walls to fuck up."

"Damn, girl," Marisol sympathized. "That is grim."

"It's the truth."

Marisol started to groom Diana's braids, trying to smooth them. "Your face is looking more normal."

"Ow," Diana complained. "Your talons are catching— Oh, shit!" She turned away quickly before he saw.

Adrian was standing on the curb, outside the school grounds.

"What?" Marisol demanded.

"My hundred percent man. Ex-hundred percent. Across the street."

Marisol spotted a slim, dark youth, leaning against a pole, looking in their direction. She whistled appreciatively.

"Don't be so obvious—damn!" Diana moaned.

"That's him? With the forearms? If he's so 'ex,' what's he doing here?"

"Maybe he's a glutton for punishment."

"So go over there," Marisol urged.

Diana hesitated. Squirming gleefully, Marisol gave her a light shove. "He's a *fox*. If you don't go I get to punish him instead."

"I don't know how you put up with me all this time."

"Get outta here!" Marisol hissed.

Reluctantly, Diana stood up and slowly walked across the street. For a moment she and Adrian stared at each other uncertainly.

"Heard you fought Ray," Adrian said quietly. "You were right. He's a fucking case. . . ."

Diana looked away, uncomfortable.

"I feel pretty stupid out here, waiting for school to be let out," Adrian commented.

"Then don't."

Adrian kept his eyes on the ground. "Right."

"So where's your woman when she doesn't have her tongue in your ear?" Diana blurted, unable to contain her anger. "Or do you only bring her out for special occasions?"

It took a long time before Adrian was able to answer. "I came here to say I'm sorry."

"For what?" Diana snorted. "Proving to your friends you can still snag the pretty girl? You got yourself a trophy now, makes you feel real big inside—"

"I don't feel too big right now. Matter of fact I feel real fucking small around you. Must be nice—"

"It's not."

Adrian shrugged. "I mean, you and me, we just met, right? We barely know each other, right?"

Stung by his cold logic, Diana stared at him. "Yeah, right. No problem. So leave."

"Maybe I don't wanna leave."

"Why?" Diana asked coldly. "You made your flimsy apology. Now you're off the hook, free to do whatever—"

"That's not all I wanted to say," Adrian blurted. "I told Karina it's not gonna work out with her. I told her I met someone who makes something happen for me." He paused and looked away. "Just cuz it's true doesn't mean I know what to do about it, okay? You got something to say about this?" he added hopefully.

She didn't answer.

Finally, he pulled her close to him. Her body stiffened, resisting.

"Hey," Adrian said softly.

"So I'm someone, huh?" Diana asked.

"Yeah. You are."

They slowly melted into each other's arms. When they kissed it was like the very first time—or the very last. . . .

When Diana arrived at the gym, Hector was in his office, reading some news clippings. He waved her inside and tossed the clippings across the desk.

"I was wrong. There's more than one of you out there," he announced. "And I hear she's *good.*"

Diana scanned the clippings as she wrapped her hands. One clipping had a photo of a female boxer holding up a trophy. The smiling woman's name was Ricki Stiles.

"She's southpaw, and she's won most of her matches 'cause of it," Hector told her, with a trace of excitement. "Sounds like more flash than power, but she's dropped some decent girls going jelly at her jab."

"Guess it feels like a right," Diana murmured, still studying the photo.

"Exactly. In my mind you can beat this girl if you train like a converted southpaw."

Hector's enthusiasm was contagious. Spurred by the prospect of a real match, Diana elevated her training. She ran four miles every morning and came to the gym early to work on her power on the heavy bag. Hector was at her side every minute.

"Keep moving, moving," he called out. He concentrated on her footwork and made her hit the heavy bag with her left hand only.

Hector devised other special training techniques to get Diana ready for the bout. He made her stand in front of a balloon suspended at chin height by an elastic rope attached to both floor and ceiling.

"It's easy to depend on your right arm for all your strength, but if you work your jab offensively you can control the bout," he explained.

Diana started boxing with the balloon. She soon learned that when she threw a punch the air would move the balloon aside. The harder she punched the faster she had to move. It was like her first time on the speedbag. She rarely hit the balloon squarely.

When she finished on the balloon, they moved to the ring. Hector tied her ankles with an elastic rope, forcing her to take small, controlled steps. Hector circled her, jabbing with his right hand. The right hand lead had a totally alien rhythm and Diana lost memory of her combinations.

Hector grinned knowingly. "Feels funny, right?"

"Yeah," Diana grunted, intent on her footwork.

"I'm Ricki," the trainer goaded, jabbing his right. "I'm Ricki, I'm Ricki. . . ."

Hector swung his mitts at her, and she slipped under them. He paused, then threw a lightning right jab. She moved her head, feinted, and caught him with a crisp right uppercut.

"Very nice," Hector congratulated her. "Very clever."

After a few more sessions the elastic rope didn't bother Diana. Hector held up his mitts in a right-hand lead, and she popped explosive combinations off them. Her feet moved in small circles, balanced. Suddenly he lunged at her and she ducked smoothly, returning a right hook.

The last thing Diana did at night was jump rope. Intently, she swung the rope from side to side, over twice—she had become one of the best in the gym. Even Cal and Adrian paused to watch her routine of tricks.

The weeks became a blur of speedbag, heavy

bag, shadowbox, spar, until finally fight day arrived.

Hector drove Diana to the White Plains Athletic Club. They waited in line with the other fighters to check in and register. Diana didn't see any other female boxers in the lobby.

"The key for you is not losing your cool," Hector said as they went inside.

Part of the gym had been set aside for weigh-ins. Diana saw a woman with short blond hair and freckled skin on one of the scales.

"That's her," Hector whispered. "Ricki Stiles."

Ricki lingered to watch Diana step onto the scale. Diana hoped she made the weight. She'd been eating more since her training had intensified. She watched the numbers tip to 126, then balance at 125.

Unlike her home gym, the White Plains A.C. had set aside locker facilities for female competitors. Diana changed and tried to warm up by shadowboxing. She had worked up a light sweat by the time Ricki entered.

The blond fighter seemed not to notice her. *Like I'm invisible or something,* Diana thought.

Hector appeared at the door. "Time!" he called.

As Diana left the room, Ricki remained stretched out on a bench, eyes closed as if asleep.

When Diana stepped into the gym she realized it was a full house. On her way to the ring she passed a table covered with gold trophies. She glanced around as she stepped through the ropes, looking for Ricki. But her opponent was still in the locker room.

"Remember, southpaw, right jab, stay cool," Hector chanted. The announcer stepped to the center of the ring. The noisy crowd gave Diana a cool reception when she was introduced.

"From Brooklyn, at one hundred twenty-five pounds with a record of one win, on a disqualification, Diana Guzman."

There was a smattering of applause. Diana looked down and saw Tiny and Adrian at ringside.

"And from right here in White Plains . . ."

A loud cheer went up as the announcer began his introduction. Ricki Stiles emerged from the locker room and strode to the ring, her local fans applauding every step.

"Don't let her psych you out," Hector warned.

". . . with a record of six straight wins, three by knockout, Ricki Stiles!"

Ricki danced around the ring as the applause grew louder.

The referee drew both fighters together and gave his instructions. "Girls, I want a good, clean fight. It's my decision if one of you needs a standing count. If you score a knockdown, go to the farthest neutral corner and stay there. Don't come out until I tell you to resume the fight. Get it?"

Both girls nodded and went back to their corners.

"Just fight your fight," Hector repeated. "South-paw, right jab, stay cool."

Diana nodded, but she was nervous. When the bell rang she came out slowly. But Ricki didn't waste any time, unleashing a fast combination that ripped through Diana's defense. Stunned, Diana stepped back, frozen with sudden panic.

Then she saw Ricki coming at her, and her trained instincts took over. Diana slipped the right jab and leaned into Ricki's body with a solid hook.

"Nice!" Hector yelled. He looked over to make sure the three judges noticed.

Ricki kept throwing flashy combinations, im-pressing the crowd with her speedy footwork. Diana had settled into the fight and countered with a couple of uppercuts. Ricki had speed but not much power. Her hook swiped Diana's jaw, but she tilted her head to absorb the impact.

Hector nodded grimly. "Good chin," he muttered. "Now bring it."

Diana slipped another hook and threw a light uppercut at the bell.

"The judges are gonna give that to Stiles 'cause they see her hands moving," Hector said, wiping sweat from Diana's face. He sprayed water into her mouth. "Remind 'em you're in there with her. Work your jab. She throws her left and leans in, that's when you unload your uppercut."

The bell rang for round two.

Again Ricki came out fast, with entertaining footwork reminiscent of Sugar Ray Leonard. The crowd cheered loudly even though her first combination missed.

Diana stared her down and landed a heavy left hook. She tried to control the circle of activity by moving with Ricki's jab and slammed another hook to her ribs.

"That's it, that's it!" Hector shouted.

Diana jammed another hook to Ricki's exposed ribcage. Ricki swung for Diana's face, but she moved aside and popped Ricki's nose hard with a right cross. Ricki came back with two quick jabs when the bell rang.

"Okay," Hector yelled, squirting water into Diana's mouth. "Your punches are making contact, your defense is strong. But you gotta stagger her. These judges love fancy footwork. They won't give you points if they don't see you slow her down."

Diana nodded, in her own world. The bell rang, and she moved quickly to the center of the ring, circling Ricki with a predatory intensity.

"You got the power!" Hector yelled. "Left hook, left hook. The more you throw the left the more she's gotta work her right."

Diana snapped her right as if it were a jab, distracting Ricki. Ricki's footwork had slowed down, and she was breathing through her mouth. Her right jab, too, had slowed. Diana threw an uppercut to the body that pushed her back.

Hector kept shouting encouragement. "Frustrate her. Give southpaw a taste of her own medicine."

The last twenty seconds of the fight belonged to Diana. She became the aggressor, landing combinations at will. She cut off Ricki's space with a jab and hook, then repeated.

"Yes, yes!" Tiny yelled, leaping to his feet.

Diana unloaded a wicked uppercut at the bell.

But as she walked back to her corner the cheers were all for Ricki.

"You did good," Hector congratulated her. Nervously, he watched the announcer collect the scorecards. Diana and Ricki stood with their trainers as the announcer took the mike.

"Ladies and gentlemen, we have a split decision," the announcer intoned. "Judge Hill scores it twenty-nine, twenty-seven, for Guzman . . ."

Ricki's fans let out a chorus of boos.

"Yes!" Hector whispered, grabbing Diana's arm. Still exhilarated from the battle, she didn't register what the announcer was saying.

"Ferrara judges twenty-nine, twenty-seven, for Stiles."

A great cheer went up among the spectators and Ricki gave them a smile.

"Anderson judges twenty-eight, twenty-seven, for Guzman."

Ricki's face fell in disbelief. "Aw, man. This isn't happening."

Diana heard the announcer's words in stunned confusion.

"And the bout goes to the winner—Diana Guzman!"

The crowd booed, stomping their feet in protest.

"You won!" Hector yelled.

I won, Diana exulted, moving across the ring to give Ricki the traditional embrace. Ricki turned her back on Diana and ranted at her trainer. "You told me she didn't have a chance!"

"You got robbed," the trainer said sadly. "That's a fact. Robbed."

Diana turned and saw Tiny and Adrian applauding. The expression on Adrian's face made her victory sweet. At that moment, amid the chaos of boos, Diana was happier than she had ever been in her life.

Chapter 11

The next day, Diana and Adrian celebrated her victory with hamburgers and a movie. Adrian called Cal, who asked him to come to the gym with Diana.

"Says he has some big news," Adrian told her as he drove to the waterfront.

When they arrived they found Hector, Cal, and Ira in the main office. Hector and Ira smiled uneasily. Cal wasn't smiling at all.

Diana looked at Hector. "So what's the big news?"

Ira answered with a wheezing cough. He dabbed his mouth with a tissue and peered at Diana. "Based on the results of your preliminary matches, you've advanced to the finals."

"Even though my first fight was stopped?"

"Yes," Ira said hoarsely. "You scored better than a lot of kids in your division."

Diana grinned. "That's great. That's really great. So who's next?"

Ira warily glanced at Adrian. Hector looked away. Suddenly Cal spoke up.

"He could destroy her, Hector!"

"Come on, Cal, you saw her with Stiles—"

Cal cut him off. "She shouldn't've advanced in the first place! That pansy ref shoulda stopped the bout with Ray cuz she wasn't fit to fight!"

"Call it dumb luck she's stuck in the ring with a scumbag who disqualifies himself," Hector said sharply. "She's fit now and that's what matters."

Adrian seemed to wake up. "What's going on here?"

Cal turned to him. "I'll tell you what. A rinky-dink operation—'scuse my candor, Ira—let this goddamn gender-blind program get outta hand!"

"You signed him up for it," Hector reminded him.

"Hector, I never thought it'd come to this!" Cal protested, glancing at Diana. "Boys are different from girls. What's so wrong about saying it out loud? *Boys are different from girls!* No girl has what it takes to be a great boxer. Neither do most boys." He threw up his hands in surrender. "I'm gonna petition the fight."

"Aw, c'mon," Hector groaned. "You're the one always complaining you can't get enough matches for your guys."

Cal looked at Ira imploringly. "You know the score, Ira. Times have changed. People want more than warriors. They want boy next door—they want TV!"

Hector folded his arms. "She advanced fair and square."

"Adrian's young, he works hard, he's a good-looking kid. Year from now he could be grooming for the pros," Cal insisted.

"Then you're pushing him," Hector declared.

Cal ignored him. "You can't humiliate my guy like this! I need your support, Ira."

The heavyset promoter shook his head. "You can file a protest, but don't ask me to get involved." He glanced at Adrian and Diana, then gave Cal a sad smile. "I will say this: let the boxers box and that'll speak for itself. You're right, Cal—times have changed."

Cal rolled his eyes to the ceiling. "Unbelievable."

Adrian looked at Diana as if she had betrayed

him, then hurried from the room. Realizing he somehow blamed her, Diana followed.

"Adrian, wait . . ."

"Hector if this happens I'm telling Adrian no mercy—you understand?" Cal was yelling as Diana ran out.

Adrian hurried down the stairs ahead of Diana. When she reached the street it was empty. Diana walked to the small alley at the side of the building. Adrian was there, pacing back and forth.

Diana watched him somberly, saying nothing.

"This is crazy," Adrian declared finally. He looked at Diana. "Cal is right. This fucks with my record."

"It's your *amateur* record," she reminded him, trying to lighten the mood. "Least we got the same disadvantage. We know each other's habits."

"Fuck!" Adrian's expression was both disgusted and indignant.

"C'mon—styles makes fights—right?" she said playfully.

Adrian scowled. "You can't do it, Diana."

"I can't?" A tiny alarm went off in her head.

"No." He looked away. "That's not what I mean. *We* can't."

171

"Why not?" Diana knew what was coming, but she hoped she was wrong.

"I won't fight you," Adrian said vehemently. "That's insane."

"You're a boxer. I'm a boxer. We're in the same weight division." Diana listed the facts even though she knew Adrian didn't care about facts right now. He was more concerned about his masculine image.

"But this is competition," Adrian said lamely.

"Yeah, and in this competition, we're all who's left," Diana reminded him with a trace of pride. Her voice softened, and she moved closer to him. "First time I saw you, I knew I wanted us to fight."

"You have lost your mind." Adrian turned and looked up at the bright patch of sky above the alley. Neither of them spoke for long moments. Then he softly snapped his fingers. "I got it—I won't make the weight."

"What?" It was Diana's turn to be indignant.

"Yeah. I'll *eat* for a fucking change," Adrian said triumphantly. "I won't fight you, and that's it."

Diana felt a flash of anger. "Who says you'll be the only one fighting?"

"I'm sorry." Adrian turned away in exasperation.

"But I haven't been training all this while to be stuck in the ring with a girl."

"Oh? Stuck with a girl," Diana repeated, temper flaring.

"Okay, how about being stuck with *you*."

Diana gave him a deadly smile. "You're afraid I might win."

"No!" Adrian snorted as if the idea was ridiculous.

"But you're gonna play it all manly and protective on me," Diana went on, fully angry now. *This isn't about me, or us,* she fumed. *This is all about him.*

"I'm just being honest," Adrian protested.

That's what they all say when they're stepping on your dream, Diana thought. She had hoped Adrian would understand. "You're no different than any other guy," she said coldly.

"What kinda guy beats up a girl that he . . . he . . ." Adrian jammed his hands into his pockets and looked away.

Suddenly Diana's anger evaporated. "That he what?" she asked softly. She had been longing for him to say it. Dreaming about it. "What?"

The answer she hoped for never came. "It's just not right. Just forget it."

"Fine," Diana said coldly. She was finished long-ing, waiting, dreaming; she was going to do it. "Think whatever the fuck you want. If you don't fight me in the match you're less of a man than you think."

Adrian gave her a sad smile. "Diana, there is no way you could beat me."

There was no more anger. And no more love. Diana felt drained of emotion as she stared at Adrian. "Maybe you're right," she said quietly. "But you haven't seen me when I get mad." She turned and walked away.

Adrian grabbed her arm. "What do you want from me, anyway? You want me to take you more seriously, is that it? That's your idea of Prince Charming?"

"Aw, please," Diana said, yanking free. "Take *yourself* more fucking seriously. Who's the one who said they love to be challenged? Love to win—"

"I won't love winning this one," Adrian said grimly.

Diana nailed him. "Then maybe you shouldn't be a boxer."

She left him there in the alley, alone and confused. He had lost something, but he still didn't know what.

Diana carefully unlocked the door to her apart-ment, ready to bolt if her father was home. Fortunately the house was empty. She saw a light in her brother's room and peeked inside. Tiny was sitting at his desk with a drawing pad.

"Hey," Diana said softly.

Tiny looked up and smiled. "Back so soon?"

"Just came to pick up some stuff."

"He won't be back till morning," Tiny said, returning to his sketch. "Night shift again."

Diana came closer and looked over his shoulder. Tiny was drawing a boldly colored version of their housing project as seen in elastic wide-angle. Diana didn't know much about art, but she could see the strength in his lines.

"That's a freaky version of home."

"Guess I dream in color." Tiny paused to admire his work. "I told Dad I'd never be a tough guy," he confided. He turned to her with a proud grin. "I'm the artistic type, I said."

Diana put a hand on his shoulder. "Good for you."

"You're the champion bruiser in the family."

Right now all I feel is bruised, Diana thought, moving to her room to pick up some fresh clothes.

Since Diana had moved in, Hector had been running with her in the mornings. But he wasn't really in shape for Diana's five-mile outings at her high school track. He stopped after two miles and leaned over with a cramp.

"Hey," Diana said, trotting back to him. "I'm just getting started with you."

He waved her off. "When you watch Adrian box, whaddya you see?"

"He's fast."

"But so are you."

"He's tall. Long reach. He's strong."

"Where's his strength?" Hector prodded.

"In his right—"

Hector beamed at her triumphantly. "You got it."

He motioned her closer and put up his fists. He started moving around her, flicking a jab. She moved her head, easily avoiding the blow. Hector kept throwing jabs, talking as they circled around.

"Adrian's got a funny habit," he told her. "Mostly he's stepping left when he uses his right hand." To illustrate he threw a jab and hook. She shifted and ducked away.

"But what about him stepping right?" she asked, still moving.

Hector followed her with fast combinations. "Well, that's just it," he explained breathlessly. "He's trained so his combinations go dead as he moves right—like he's not used to it. When he and Ray were fighting he led the whole thing with his left foot. 'Course Ray took it lying down, couldn't keep his head on straight." Hector slowed his combination so Diana could see what he meant. "If you throw off his movement to the left, he loses his speed—and you can slip inside that reach of his."

Exhausted, Hector dropped his hands.

"He said there's no way I can beat him," Diana said, looking away.

"Well, that's what he's gotta say," Hector told her gently. He wiped his thumb across her forehead and tasted her sweat. "You're not drinking enough water."

Chapter 12

Diana used her training to block out all the pain, loss, and loneliness crammed into her short life.

Hector seemed to be the only one who understood what boxing meant to her. For the first time she had a sense of real purpose. Her trainer worked her hard, and when fight night came, Diana was ready.

The finals were being staged at the auditorium of Our Lady of Mount Carmel, which could accommodate a big crowd. Any worries Ira might have harbored were put to rest by the large number of early arrivals for the event.

Diana waited in the priest's rectory, shadowboxing to warm up. She could hear the announcer's voice cutting through the loud murmur of the crowd.

"Ladies and gentlemen, please rise for our national anthem."

As the referee began to sing, Hector came into the rectory. He seemed more nervous than Diana as he watched her circle, bob, and punch. Despite his apprehension, Hector noted Diana's improvement over the past few months. No longer awkward, she moved like a panther; swift and lethal.

"How you feeling?" he asked softly.

Diana sliced a left hook. "Like I got nothing to lose."

"Okay then," Hector said briskly as he started taping her hands.

Diana spread her fingers in a star. "Leave me some room."

Just then the door opened and Cal stepped inside, followed by Adrian. Diana's belly did a soft flip when she saw him. For a moment they locked eyes, then Adrian walked past to the other side of the rectory.

Hector leaned close to her face. "Inside, you know him?"

"Yeah," Diana answered, aware of what was coming.

"How's he fight?"

They'd repeated the little ritual countless times. "He's always stepping left and relies on his right for all his power," Diana recited dutifully. "Leading him to my left will break his rhythm. His jab gets a little low, but his right cross could knock me out."

Hector crouched in front of her and looked into her eyes. "Inside—you know yourself?"

Diana paused. It was the first time he had asked. "I do," she said finally. But she wasn't really sure.

Hector squeezed her shoulder. "Then that's all you need."

Outside the rectory door the crowd was cheering. As Diana entered the auditorium, the noise swept over her. "Welcome, ladies and gentlemen, to history in the making. . . ." the announcer called. "New York's first Gender-Blind Amateur Boxing Finals . . ."

As the announcer continued, Diana walked down the aisle to her corner, closely followed by Hector. She was barely conscious of what the announcer was saying. The one thing on her mind was the fight. It was her salvation from her father's brutality, her mother's suicide, and her own grinding struggle to find her place in a world that had no place for her.

Adrian entered the ring as the announcer was

thanking their commercial sponsors. When he climbed through the black ropes, their eyes met.

On impulse Diana smiled, and he looked away.

"In the green shorts," the announcer began, "weighing in at one hundred twenty-five pounds, nineteen years old and a *Daily News* contender—let's welcome Adrian Abreu to the featherweight finals."

A loud cheer rippled through the crowd. Adrian lifted his gloves.

"And in the lovely lilac shorts," the announcer continued, "weighing in at one hundred twenty-four pounds, eighteen years old, new to the finals and a real trooper, ladies and gentlemen—clap your hands for Diana Guzman!"

A few boos filtered through the polite applause. Diana glanced into the crowd and spotted her brother in the second row. Tiny looked worried.

Diana went to the center of the ring for her instructions. The ref held both fighters by the shoulders, while he issued the standard warnings. Diana looked into Adrian's eyes but he instantly turned away.

They went back to their corners. Hector stood face-to-face with Diana, giving her last minute instructions. "Lead him with your jab. Keep moving to your left—force him to come to you."

Across the ring, Adrian was hastily conferring with his trainer. "I can't go through with this, Cal."

"Yes, you can," Cal assured him wearily. "Just do some damage in this round and it'll be short and sweet."

The bell rang and both fighters advanced, touching gloves. They were both hesitant for the first few seconds until Diana threw the first jab. Adrian bobbed out of the way, and for the next two minutes they went to work; circling, throwing punches. To Cal's frustration Diana landed as often as Adrian— at the same time avoiding his right.

She wasn't really aggressive, and Adrian tried to take advantage of that. Graceful and fluid, he kept hammering combinations while she bobbed and slipped away. Suddenly Diana sprang and landed a solid right to Adrian's jaw, just before the bell.

"Pick up the pace," Hector said excitedly as he squirted water into her mouth. "You're doing good by leading him."

"I need to go for his body more," Diana said, almost to herself.

"But keep it loose, keep it loose," Hector implored,

rubbing her shoulders. "You're all hunched up here."

In Adrian's corner Cal was impatient. "So she's got defensive skills, big deal. Take her out and finish her!"

The bell rang for the second round. Both fighters sprang to the center, eager to engage. Diana threw a jab that Adrian countered with a furious right hand. She staggered back, completely taken by surprise.

Adrian slammed a combination to her gut, and she twisted, reeling for a moment. She countered with an equally damaging combination, and they locked arms. The ref pried them apart, and they went to work again.

Diana slipped his jab, but a powerful right smacked her eye. Instinctively she threw an uppercut to his belly and he fell back against the ropes. Adrian swung for her eye again but she blocked with her right and threw a compact left jab and hook combination to his chin. The crowd roared at the flurry of action.

They fell into a clinch, and when the ref separated them Diana's face was smeared with blood. Hector glanced at the judges. One of them was shaking his head.

When the bell rang both fighters staggered to their corners. The ref leaned over the ropes conferring with the disapproving judge. As Diana sat down, Hector leaned, trying to hear.

"I'm not gonna stop it, Bert," the ref was saying. "They're exchanging blows—just like it says in the rulebook."

"Sit still," Hector told Diana gently. "I gotta work on this eye."

He quickly wiped the blood from the cut above her eye. It was deep. He applied salve and pressure, trying to close the wound.

Diana groaned. "He keeps opening it up."

"And he'll keep trying," Hector warned, lifting his voice above the noise. "He knows you want to protect this. *Don't* hide it from him. His jab is getting low and his swings are wild—that leaves him open. Find a way in and go for his brain every chance you get."

"Okay."

"Your punches make contact, but you got to swarm him more." Hector crouched eye to eye in front of her. "I don't care who this guy is to you. Don't be afraid to hurt him! Put your life behind that hook of yours and he could take a fall."

The bell rang for the final round. Diana shuffled forward and threw a halfhearted jab. Hector scowled. That wasn't what he was looking for. Diana seemed to have forgotten everything she knew. She shielded herself and let Adrian lead her to her left.

Adrian immediately went for her face. Diana slipped and countered. When their eyes met there was a flash of recognition. She glimpsed his fierce animal intensity—and realized how badly he wanted to win. And how desperately *she* wanted to win.

In that instant everything fell away: the screams of the crowd, the angry throb of her wounded eye, the smell of blood and sweat, the ragged exhaustion tearing at her lungs, and she knew she could beat him.

Adrian attacked with swift combinations and Diana moved faster. Her hands found a rhythm that matched his while her feet worked him to her right. Her left uppercut swatted his ribs, leaving a red welt.

Sensing blood, the crowd leaped to its feet. Tiny looked around and saw his father standing near the trophy table. The spectators roared, and Tiny turned back to the ring.

Diana kept leading Adrian to his right, and he couldn't adjust. He swung a wide hook, leaning forward, and Diana cracked his jaw with a short left hook. Stunned, Adrian stopped.

Frozen in the moment, Diana saw she could knock him out, the love of her life.

Hector saw it, too. And Tiny. And Sandro. For a split second Diana teetered on a rope between uncertainty and triumph. Then she moved.

Diana jammed two hard uppercuts into Adrian's nose and he staggered from the stinging shock to his brain. Slowly he fell to the floor.

Cal pounded on the ring apron, grimacing in horror. "Up! Get up!"

Still dazed, Adrian pulled himself to his feet. The ref got in front of him and began a standing count. "Three . . . four . . . five . . ."

By eight Adrian had recovered and nodded emphatically to show he was fine. The referee motioned both fighters to the center of the ring. They resumed fighting.

Adrian came at Diana like an express train, and for the final ten seconds of the bout they exchanged a dazzling flurry of blows. Toe to toe, their fists blurred, their bodies bobbed and twisted, locked in a violent dance.

"Take her out!" Cal pleaded through the crowd's roar. "Take her out!"

The bell rang and they fell into an exhausted embrace. Then Adrian broke away and glared at her, his stony anger laced with sorrow.

"Satisfied?" he muttered.

As Adrian turned away Hector scrambled into the ring. The trainer hugged her and raised her arm in a triumphant salute. The spectators applauded and Diana saw Tiny jumping up and down excitedly.

The announcer stared at Diana, mopping his face with a handkerchief as the judges filled out their scorecards. They solemnly turned in their decisions. The announcer took the cards and lifted his mike.

Diana glanced at Adrian's corner, but he had his back turned.

"Ladies and gentlemen, we have a unanimous decision. The amateur featherweight champ in these finals is—Diana Guzman!"

Delirious with joy, Diana pumped her arms high in the air and walked a winner's circle around the ring. The crowd began chanting rhythmically for her. Tiny came to the edge of the ring, tears streaming down his face.

"I can't believe you sometimes!" he shouted. "You did it! You're a winner!"

As the crowd continued to cheer, Diana went to Adrian's corner. Cal said nothing and Adrian walked away, still dazed. As Diana watched him leave the ring she spotted her father among the spectators. Sandro was clapping his hands. Applauding her.

Hector came up and put his arm around her. "In all my life I never been so proud," he whispered hoarsely. "Never."

Diana smiled at Hector. "Yeah" was all she could say. But her heart was flooded with conflicting emotions.

Later, Diana sat alone in the locker room listening to the slow drip of the faucet echoing in the silence. Her hands were still wrapped and she slumped on her stool, taking deep breaths. In a way she felt as if she had been knocked out and was slowly recovering her senses. The wild adrenaline of the fight had drained away, leaving her empty.

The sadness stole over her like the moon's shadow over the sun, eclipsing her victory elation, and Diana began to weep, the hot tears dissolving the caked blood around her eye.

She was born to lose everyone she loved in this world.

Early the next morning Adrian went back to the auditorium at Our Lady of Mount Carmel. He hadn't slept much, still rerunning every punch of the previous night's fight. The large room was empty except for the janitor cleaning up near the ring. Adrian walked past the janitor and climbed into the ring.

He moved slowly, reenacting the fight, as if trying to decipher the code of events leading to his loss. He threw some combinations, stepping to his left. In his mind he heard the crowd roaring, Cal shouting "take her out!"

Adrian stepped right and threw a right hook, wild and a little off-balance. As he leaned forward he remembered crashing into Diana's left hook.

"Heard there was a great fight here last night."

Adrian turned and saw the janitor leaning on his broom.

"Boxers fighting something fierce," the janitor went on. "Heard a girl knocked down a guy."

"Sounds like one for the books," Adrian agreed.

The janitor resumed his sweeping. "Whatever it takes to make a fight worth watching is what I say. These days it's hard to find the right match. . . ."

His words chimed in Adrian's mind like a ring bell. Adrian recalled having said the very same thing to a girl he loved, not so long ago. "Yeah," he said, climbing through the ropes. "Yeah, it is."

Diana had come down early to the Brooklyn Athletic Club to clean up the supply closet that served as her locker. As she moved some rotten mops away from the wall she discovered a window, covered with years of grime.

She started rubbing the dirt from the glass, and a shaft of sunlight cut through the gloom. A shuffling sound drew her attention. She turned and saw Adrian standing at the doorway.

"Someone really worked you over," he said quietly.

Startled, Diana's hand went to her swollen eye.

Adrian smiled. "You got a deadly hook."

"Your right cross is no powder puff."

He nodded, then looked away. "I gave you everything I had."

"Me, too." Diana became aware of her racing heartbeat.

"Boxing, going pro—I want it to be my ticket out, you know?" Adrian shook his head, eyes still averted. "I gave you an opening, it was stupid."

Diana moved closer to where he could see her face. "But that's what happens. You just—take advantage," she said, as if explaining the simplest thing in the world.

"Yeah." He shrugged. "Now I lose your respect, huh?"

"No."

"After last night? Come on." Adrian turned away.

Diana followed him. "Adrian, you boxed with me like I was any other guy! You didn't back down or give me a break or take it easy on me. Man, you heard that crowd—we were toe to toe and they loved it! You threw down and showed *me* respect. Don't you see what that means?"

Adrian looked at her solemnly. "That life with you is war?"

"Maybe. Maybe life is war, period."

"You said it." Adrian took her hand and paused, staring at the raw, bloody skin around her knuckles.

"Hector wraps them too tight."

The voices of boxers arriving for their morning workout filtered through the brief silence. Adrian lifted Diana's hand and softly kissed her knuckles.

"Life's been a mess since I met you," he whispered. He hated losing to her—losing her might be more than he could bear. "So, you gonna dump me now?"

Diana nodded, eyes brimming. "Yeah."

"You promise?"

A slow smile spread across her tear-streaked face. "Cross my heart."

As they kissed, Diana kicked the door shut. But she knew it was only the beginning of a long, hard fight. . . .

Girlfight

The Story Behind the Movie

"I've always been interested in the classic story of a nobody who becomes a somebody," says writer/director Karyn Kusama. "Whether it's Terry Mallory in *On the Waterfront* or, more recently, Tony Manero in *Saturday Night Fever*, I've always been drawn to these characters. The idea of a personal growth through physical transformation fascinated me, and I thought it would make an even more interesting story if the main character were a woman. But *Girlfight* is about more than boxing in the same way that *Saturday Night Fever* is about more than disco."

Boxing Is Brains Over Brawn

Kusama chose the world of boxing as the metaphor for her powerful, award-winning story based on personal experience. A fan, Kusama started boxing in her early twenties and found it fascinating on many levels. The solitude of training in contrast with the immediacy of confronting an opponent in the ring, the physicality of the sport compared to the intense concentration and focus required—all these things inspired Kusama to explore the sport in her first feature film.

"Boxing is very intimate," she says. "It's strangely moving to see two people agree to be in a ring together to fight each other, yet it's necessarily tragic—somebody loses and somebody wins. I find it one of the purest sports, a very powerful confrontation between you and your opponent." However, Kusama adds, "In boxing, as in any sport, you are confronting yourself."

Kusama found boxing a rich backdrop against which to explore a specific time in everyone's life fraught with confusion and misdirected energy: adolescence. "Adolescence is so chaotic," explains Kusama. "Your hormones are in overdrive, and life is such a roller coaster of feeling. It can be such a creative time—if all that energy is harnessed. But most kids don't find an outlet where they can shape and focus all that energy. In boxing, one can focus and channel not just the physical energy but the creative energy, too."

* * *

When You're Not Training, Someone Else Is Training to Kick Your Ass

The physicality of boxing and its wordless form of confrontation also seemed remarkably appropriate for adolescence. "We tend to want to gloss over the messiness of adolescence and daily life. I definitely wanted to try to avoid that in the script," Kusama says.

Instead, the evolution of the main character, Diana Guzman, is seen mainly through her progress at the gym. Her growing self-confidence is evident in the increasingly relaxed way she carries herself, looking less like she is coiled and ready to strike as she walks down the hallways of her high school. Part of Diana's newfound confidence comes from letting go of her father's low expectations for her and moving beyond them into her own expectations for herself.

"It's a common story that we are most angry and most difficult when we're boxed in by expectations—either of ourselves, our family, or society at large. I think men and women alike feel that pressure to be somebody other than who they are," Kusama says.

* * *

Champions Are Made, Not Born

In writing *Girlfight*, Karyn Kusama draws a parallel between life in the ring and the ongoing struggle to become fully involved in one's life outside of the ring. "More than anything," she says, "the story is about the struggle to grow and survive."

About the Author

A native of Brooklyn, **Frank Lauria** is the author of the Minstrel Books tie-ins *Alaska* and *The Mask of Zorro*. For other publishers he has novelized *End of-Days, Pitch Black,* and *Dark City*. He has published eleven novels for adults, including three bestsellers. He has written magazine articles and book reviews and has been an advertising and publishing copy writer and a book editor. Frank Lauria currently teaches a writing workshop in San Francisco, where he lives.